You're About to Become a

Privileged

Woman.

INTRODUCING
PAGES & PRIVILEGES™.

It's our way of thanking you for buying
our books at your favorite retail store.

GET ALL THIS FREE

WITH JUST ONE PROOF OF PURCHASE:

◆ **Hotel Discounts** up
to 60% at home and
abroad ◆ **Travel Service**
- Guaranteed lowest
published airfares
plus 5% cash back
on tickets ◆ **$25 Travel Voucher**

$50 VALUE

◆ **Sensuous Petite Parfumerie** collection

◆ **Insider Tips Letter**
with sneak previews
of upcoming books

You'll get a *FREE personal card, too.*
It's your passport to all these benefits— and to
even more great gifts & benefits to come!

There's no club to join. No purchase commitment. No obligation.

Enrollment Form

☐ *Yes!* I WANT TO BE A *P*RIVILEGED *W*OMAN.

Enclosed is one *PAGES & PRIVILEGES*™ Proof of Purchase from any Harlequin or Silhouette book currently for sale in stores (Proofs of Purchase are found on the back pages of books) and the store cash register receipt. Please enroll me in *PAGES & PRIVILEGES*™. Send my Welcome Kit and FREE Gifts -- and activate my FREE benefits -- immediately.

More great gifts and benefits to come like these luxurious Truly Lace and L'Effleur gift baskets.

NAME (please print)
_____

ADDRESS _____ APT. NO _____

CITY _____ STATE _____ ZIP/POSTAL CODE _____

┌─────────────────────────────────────┐
│ 📖 PROOF OF PURCHASE   │
│ Pages & Privileges™   SAMPLE ONLY   │
└─────────────────────────────────────┘

Please allow 6-8 weeks for delivery. Quantities are limited. We reserve the right to substitute items. Enroll before October 31, 1995 and receive one full year of benefits.

NO CLUB! NO COMMITMENT!
*Just one purchase brings you great **Free Gifts** and **Benefits!***
(More details in back of this book.)

Name of store where this book was purchased_____

Date of purchase_____

Type of store:

☐ Bookstore   ☐ Supermarket   ☐ Drugstore

☐ Dept. or discount store (e.g. K-Mart or Walmart)

☐ Other (specify)_____

Which Harlequin or Silhouette series do you usually read?
_____

Complete and mail with one Proof of Purchase and store receipt to:

U.S.: *PAGES & PRIVILEGES*™, P.O. Box 1960, Danbury, CT 06813-1960

Canada: *PAGES & PRIVILEGES*™, 49-6A The Donway West, P.O. 813, North York, ON M3C 2E8   **PRINTED IN U.S.A**

She wasn't used to having a man in her kitchen.

She was used to moving around the big empty house by herself. That had to be the reason for her disorientation.

Yeah, but why are your hormones hopscotching like crazy? an inner voice mocked.

Dina had to pause a minute, clear her head, think. Gabe had saved her life. Maybe she could safely classify him as a friend?

She eyed the width of his shoulders and felt an accompanying weakness in her knees. She ditched the friends theory. Friendship didn't account for her stampeding pulse.

Smoldering awareness was swirling between them. And Dina swallowed. Hard. Gabriel might have saved her from a fire…

But who was going to save her from the fire *he* had started in *her?*

Dear Reader,

This month, Silhouette Romance has a wonderful lineup—sure to add love and laughter to your sunny summer days and sultry nights. Marie Ferrarella starts us off with another FABULOUS FATHER in *The Women in Joe Sullivan's Life*. Sexy Joe Sullivan was an expert on *grown* women, but when he suddenly finds himself raising three small nieces, he needs the help of Maggie McGuire—and finds himself falling for her womanly charms as well as her maternal instinct! Cassandra Cavannaugh has plans for her own BUNDLE OF JOY in Julianna Morris's *Baby Talk*. And Jake O'Connor had no intention of being part of them. Can true love turn Mr. Wrong into a perfect father—and husband for Cassie?

Dorsey Kelley spins another thrilling tale for WRANGLERS AND LACE in *Cowboy for Hire*. Bent Murray thought his rodeo days were behind him, until sassy cowgirl Kate Monahan forced him to face his past—and her place in his heart. Handsome Michael Damian gets more than he bargained for in Christine Scott's *Imitation Bride*. Lacey Keegan was only pretending to be his fiancée, but now that wedding plans were snowballing, he began wishing that their make-believe romance was real.

Two more stories with humor and love round out the month in *Second Chance at Marriage* by Pamela Dalton, and *An Improbable Wife* by debut author Sally Carleen.

Happy Reading!

Anne Canadeo

Senior Editor, Silhouette Romance

Please address questions and book requests to:
Silhouette Reader Service
U.S.: 3010 Walden Ave., P.O. Box 1325, Buffalo, NY 14269
Canadian: P.O. Box 609, Fort Erie, Ont. L2A 5X3

SECOND CHANCE AT MARRIAGE

Pamela Dalton

Silhouette
R O M A N C E™
Published by Silhouette Books
America's Publisher of Contemporary Romance

To Mom
I wish to thank the following people for their help with this book—any irregularities are the result of my overzealous imagination and not my sources:
Nancy Pieri, Country Crocks; my friends at
Robinson Ransbottom Pottery; Bruce Boxrucker,
Chief of Cottage Grove Volunteer Fire Department.

 SILHOUETTE BOOKS

ISBN 0-373-19100-6

SECOND CHANCE AT MARRIAGE

Books by Pamela Dalton

Silhouette Romance

The Prodigal Husband #957
Second Chance at Marriage #1100

PAMELA DALTON

says, "My teacher's number-one complaint when I was in school was that I was a 'dreamer.' I also liked to tuck a romance novel inside my open history book when I was supposed to be studying. My mother would check on me to make sure I was doing my schoolwork and, alas, could only see the propped open history book.

"My husband claims he taught me everything I know about romance. He's my hero in every sense of the word. My children—Betsy and Peter—are very tolerant of their mother who hears voices in her head and talks to herself.

"I like reading, rock 'n' roll music and Mickey Mouse. I've traveled from Europe—we were in East Germany shortly after the Wall came down—to Jamaica and many points in between."

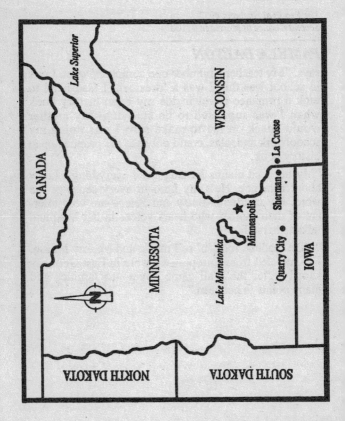

Prologue

The woman in black chuckled as she stood wrapped in the night shadows, watching the red-hot flames storm through the aging building. Nothing could stop them—she'd made sure of it. Even the new fire engine, the pride and joy of the volunteer fire department, couldn't deter the bold tongues of destruction.

Revenge was within her grasp.

The screaming of the sirens sang in her ears as the raging fire drew the cries and presence of nearly every man, woman and child. *Fools!* In their rush toward the hot, mocking flames, nobody saw her.

For once she didn't mind. She was used to being ignored and overlooked, despite the fact she—and she alone—kept the town running smoothly. For years she'd raged silently against the town's blindness.

Until tonight.

Tonight belonged to her, and she would finally reap the credit she so rightly deserved. It was time people recognized her authority and power.

Tonight she would get rid of her antagonist once and for all.

The townsfolk were stupid not to see Dina Paxton for what she was. A pretty face with no substance.

Woe be to them for their foolishness.

Soon the townspeople would understand their darling angel was the one who had caused all of this pain and terror.

What would precious Dina look like burned and scarred? The ugly vision was almost beautiful to the woman in black.

What would Dina Paxton look like dead?

The woman in black decided she liked that image best of all.

Chapter One

The muffled sound was barely discernible above the wailing sirens, but Dina Cassidy Paxton could have sworn she heard something coming from inside the burning farm-and-feed store.

There it was again.

A whimper?

Or had she imagined it?

There shouldn't be anyone in there. The old feed store had been empty for years. Panic and hysteria echoed through the streets behind her as her fellow fire fighters rushed to surround the blazing inferno. She edged closer to the building, craning her head and trying to block out the noises. Her hands clutched the fire hose, bracing for the sudden surge of water that would come at any second.

She heard it again.

A howl. Long and moaning.

Someone was trapped in the store. For a second, she froze as the fear paralyzed her. Then she was in motion. Thrusting her end of the hose into another fire fighter's hands, she ran. The store would collapse soon. One explosion had already flattened the back of the building.

She couldn't let anyone die. Not again. Her hands automatically checked to make sure her air pack was strapped to her back.

"There's someone in there," she yelled without breaking stride.

"Dina!"

She ignored the shout coming from behind her as she cleared the doorway. Her gaze raked the barren room. Debris, trash and old timber littered the floor. She didn't see anyone. Through an open doorway, flames gobbled ancient wood, showing no mercy. It was only a matter of time before the fire consumed the entire building. She had to act quickly.

"Dina, what's going on?" Tim Gimble charged through the doorway behind her, lugging the fire hose.

A moan came from overhead.

"He's upstairs." Dina frantically searched the room. The fire was advancing toward the staircase on her right. "Clear me a path."

Tim turned loose a spray of water. "Hurry! I'm not sure how long I can keep it back. The whole building's about to go!"

Within seconds, Dina was up the steps. Thick, blinding smoke shrouded her. She couldn't see a damn thing.

Panic surged.

Where was he? Was she too late? She refused to contemplate defeat.

"Anybody here?" she screamed and then choked, grabbing her face mask.

A whine sounded on her left. She turned.

Boom! The building shook. The floor shifted. She struggled to keep her balance.

"Dina!" Tim's panicked voice sounded far away. "We've got to get out of here!"

The flames circled her. Fear made her take one final plunge. All she had to do was grab the person hidden in the smoke. Adrenaline raced. She leaped toward the corner where the whine had come from and found what she was looking for.

Then the floor dipped.

Wood groaned ...

Cracked ...

Suddenly she hurtled downward. She twisted her body and took the full weight of the fall.

Aaugh! She gasped for breath. Her head swam as blackness hovered close.

"Fire fighter down!"

Dina thought she heard the scream. Or maybe she was dead and dreaming. But then she wouldn't hear the hiss and roar of the fire, would she? She wouldn't feel the intense heat.

Fire surrounded her. Hot. Vicious. Merciless.

The burden in her arms whimpered.

Instinct took over. *She had to move. She had to get them out of here.* She rolled, guessing the direction where safety beckoned. She hit the wall, dislodging her mask. Her lungs filled and burned. Her muscles were weakening. With her last bit of strength, she heaved herself to her knees. Clutching her bundle, she crawled, trying to ignore the pressure pounding inside her head.

The scared victim in her arms struggled.

"Please, sweetheart. Stay calm. We're almost free!" She whispered through her burning throat, not knowing if the poor little fella heard the words or not. He started to fight her. Her grip tightened. No, she couldn't lose him! If he continued to fight her, she didn't think she'd have the strength to save him. Flames reached for her. Desperately, she reached for her mask and slipped it over his head.

She staggered to her feet and dived through the door. She stumbled as strong, powerful arms reached and grabbed her.

"What in the hell are you trying to do? Kill yourself and everyone else with your foolish stunts?" The furious growl cut through the haze clouding her head.

Dina's eyes cracked open, but her words of thanks died as she recognized the hard face glaring down at her. Oh Lord, why did it have to be him?

His face blurred.

Under their own volition, her limbs collapsed, and she dropped straight into his arms.

He caught her close. And for a moment, she found delirious comfort in hearing the steady, purposeful beat of his heart next to her cheek.

The last thing she remembered seeing was his dark expression swimming with a mixture of anger, pain and fear. She had this crazy urge to apologize. Her lips couldn't move, however.

Then she gave up the struggle to analyze the man's anger and slipped into the blackness.

"What in the hell did you think you were doing?" The fire chief loomed over his desk and glared at his daughter-in-law. "Do you have a death wish?"

Dina straightened in the chair, the soot and smoke still clinging to her face, skin and clothes. The terror of those endless minutes five hours earlier lingered like ominous clouds in her own mind. She'd managed to recover from her fall and narrow escape, but it wasn't an experience she'd soon forget. And by the look on JD's face, he wasn't going to allow her to forget her near-death experience, either.

She raked a hand through her damp curly hair. "I couldn't ignore that someone might be trapped inside a burning building, could I?"

JD rubbed the back of his neck, as if to ease a great tension. "You came storming out of the building carrying an old dog who was using *your* air mask. Your mask is never supposed to be shared unless it's with another fire fighter."

"Hulk didn't deserve to burn to death."

"He was a blind old dog! You might have been doing that poor critter a favor."

She knew JD didn't mean to be cruel. His harshness stemmed from his concern and love for her. But in her heart, she knew she'd take the same course of action again if she was faced with a similar set of circumstances. She couldn't stand the thought that someone might be killed in a fire as her husband, Jerry, had been on that horrible night three years ago.

Upsetting JD was not something she wanted to do, either. She softened her voice. "I didn't know what was trapped inside that store, J.D. It could have been a child. Or it could have been Ralph searching for his dog. I couldn't ignore that possibility, could I?"

JD's sigh filled the room. A big teddy bear of a man with pure white hair and a gruff voice, he was usually even-tempered. It was one of the many reasons he'd been Sherman, Minnesota's fire chief for fifteen years. Few things rattled him...until now. She hadn't seen him this upset since Jerry's death.

"Did anyone see anything unusual before the fire?" she asked.

JD shook his head. "No one's come forward with any solid information." His expression became even darker.

They'd been fortunate the building had stood apart and hadn't burned down the rest of Main Street.

As she watched her father-in-law pace his office, a small room off to the side of the garage that housed all of Sherman's fire equipment, she thought about the terrible fire and its implications. They'd been lucky no one had perished.

The fire had been too determined, too ferocious, feeding off terrible explosions. A discarded cigarette would not have sparked that kind of blaze. The last explosion had been as deadly as a knife to the heart.

She hadn't witnessed anything so dangerous except for the fire six months ago that had claimed the deserted machine shop. That hadn't been a normal fire, either. The investigators had determined it was the handiwork of an arsonist. But no one had been caught.

Was there a connection between the two fires?

Six months ago, she'd made an offer to buy the old machine shop, hoping to remodel it and turn it into a craft store. The arsonist-set fire that destroyed the shop put her business plans on hold—until two days ago when she'd placed a bid on the farm-and-feed store. Now only a charred wall remained. Was it a coincidence the two buildings she had wanted were suddenly no longer in existence?

She wanted to believe the fires were an accident. Her hometown, tucked into the sheltering bluffs along the great Mississippi River, only had ten buildings in their downtown. Now only eight of those properties still remained in existence. Both the old machine shop and the farm-and-feed store had been empty. Now they were both gone. Why would anyone want to risk destroying Sherman?

No one deserved this.

The townsfolk were compassionate human beings—good solid citizens. She'd known them all her life, and owed them more than she could ever repay. Until recently, their worst crime was a collective lack of imagination. The town had some unusual personalities, but what town didn't?

She hated the helplessness besieging her. She looked up into JD's face for the answers that eluded her. "Maybe it was just an accident."

"Perhaps. We'll have to wait and see what the investigators come up with." JD looked as frustrated as she felt. He threw down his pencil and regarded her with tired eyes that made him look older than his sixty-three years. "You're the best-trained volunteer I've got, Dina. But if you pull another stunt like you did last night, I'll have to suspend you from the department. You not only put yourself in danger, you put every other volunteer at risk. They can't do their job if they have to worry about you. My job is to make sure that all of my volunteers stay alive and well. And that includes you."

"JD—" she started to protest.

He cut her off. "I wonder if it's not time for you to quit and move on."

Stunned disbelief rocked through her. If anyone else had made such an outrageous suggestion, she would have tossed his words back into his face. But this was JD. He knew what being a volunteer fire fighter meant to her.

She abruptly stood up, shaking her head almost violently. "You were the one who suggested I join the department three years ago. Why would you suggest I quit now after such a devastating fire?"

JD's gaze shifted to a stack of papers on his desk. She got a feeling he knew something that he wasn't telling her. He tapped his fingers on the desk and met her gaze again. "Three years ago, you needed something to help you heal. Now it's time to get on with your life."

She raised her palms, at a loss to understand the purpose of this conversation. "I have a life. I'm a member of the town council. I'm a scout leader. I'm—" she started to recite the list.

JD cut her off with an impatient wave of his hand. "Quit all those organizations and what would you have, honey?"

He was obviously more upset about last night's close call than she realized. She rounded the desk and stood in front of him. Her hand reached over and touched his sleeve. "I'm sorry I scared you last night. I won't apologize for saving Hulk, but I promise to take more precautions in the future. I don't want anyone else getting hurt because of me."

"I know." A sad smile crossed his face. "Always thinking of everyone else first, aren't you, honey?"

She grimaced. "I'm not a saint."

"You're the daughter I never had, Dina." He paused for a moment and cleared the hoarseness from his voice. "Jerry's been dead a long time. Isn't it time you started dating again?"

She stiffened at the reminder. Jerry had been her husband and JD's only child. One day he'd been there, her best friend and lifetime partner. The next day he was gone. "Why are you bringing this up now?"

"I want to see you happy."

She forced a tired smile on her face. "I am happy. My life couldn't be any fuller." She loved JD and her Aunt Wally, and she cared deeply about her friends. Those were the relationships she counted on now to make her life complete. They were enough. She had made sure of that.

And being a fire fighter gave her life a sense of purpose. She was committed to helping others.

JD planted his hands on the desk and drilled her with his no-nonsense stare. "Being busy doesn't take the place of having one's own family. What about getting married and having children?''

She tried to cover up her pang of regret by making a stab at lightness. "Do you have a sudden desire to be a grandpa?"

"I'd make a damn good one, don't you think?"

A tightness closed around Dina's heart. If only she could give JD what he wanted. Her former father-in-law would make a wonderful grandfather. She could almost picture him carrying a small child on his big, wide shoulders.

She stared up into his gentle face. "JD, I—"

He shook his head. "Don't answer me now. Just give some thought to what I said."

She knew the paltry smile creeping across her lips wasn't what JD was looking for, but it was the best she could do at the moment. She'd learned from the worst way possible that happy-ever-after was a futile fantasy that didn't exist for her. "I'd do anything in the world for you, JD. But getting married again is out of the question." She shook her head and tried to coax a smile from him with a bit of humor. "If you want children to bounce on your bony knee, why don't you get married again and have your own?"

Her father-in-law grunted with dissatisfaction before relenting and allowing a half smile to ease some of the tension from his face. "Okay, I'll keep my mouth shut for now. But remember, you're the only family I have left, and I don't want to lose you, too."

She walked over and gave him a heartfelt hug. "I plan to hang around for many years to come." She picked up the jacket she'd dropped across the chair. "I'd better shower before this soot sticks to my face forever. I need to stop over and check on Ralph's dog before I head home."

"Some man would love all the special attention you're awarding to that old man and his damn dog," JD said.

Dina chose to ignore his remark. She started toward the door. "I just hope my pottery driver arrives today because I'm getting low on my inventory. I need to finish painting two big orders of crocks."

JD's voice stopped her. "Speaking of your crocks, have you found anyone to help you cart and carry your pottery?"

She shook her head. "I thought Vic Bartels's son might be able to do it, but he's taken a job at the hardware store. Besides, he's back in school and I need someone who can be ready at a moment's notice. I never know when the pottery driver is going to make his deliveries."

"Gabe Randolph might be able to help you out."

"Gabe Randolph?" She frowned. The distinct memory from last night's fire crowded into her head, and she recalled Gabe Randolph's hard and very angry face before she passed out. "He's got a job. Why would he want a handyman job?"

Gabe, the son of an old army buddy of JD's, had moved into Sherman about three months ago. Although the rest of the town was giving rave reviews to his newly opened restaurant, she hadn't felt a strong desire to get friendly with the big, broad-shouldered man with dark, mesmerizing eyes—even if he had pulled her from Death's jaws just a few hours ago.

JD sat on the corner of his desk. "Last night's fire put Gabe out of a home. He was renting an apartment next door to the feed store. The structure is still standing, but the water damage caused the roof to cave in. It's uninhabitable." He watched her face closely. "Gabe's renovating the top floor above the restaurant for an apartment, but it's got a rickety fire escape that needs to be replaced. The upper story doesn't meet fire code, and he's not going to be able to move in for several months."

"I don't run a rooming house." Gabe Randolph's living problems weren't any of her concern. "I only need someone to transport my crocks from the shed to the workroom and then to assist the driver when he comes with my load of pots."

"You need a handyman, and everyone in town who has a moment to spare is helping with the cleanup after the fires." When she didn't respond, he added, "You and Gabe can help each other out. This would be a perfect arrangement for both of you.''

A blanket of uneasiness began to descend upon her. She hadn't had a man live with her since Jerry and Gramps died, and she knew with absolute certainty she wasn't ready to share her home again. Especially *not* with Gabe Randolph. There was something about him that made her want to keep a safe distance between them. ''Why can't he stay with you or someone else?''

JD shuffled a few papers on his desk, and then looked up at her. ''Gabe's too big to sleep on my lumpy sofa bed for two months. And there isn't a single house to rent in town right now.'' He walked around his desk and stood directly in front of her. ''You'd be getting a heck of a bargain. Gabe's pretty handy with tools. He might be able to fix your forklift.''

A seed of suspicion took root in her mind. ''Why do I have the feeling you've already talked to him about this arrangement?''

''I might have mentioned it to him.'' JD accompanied her to the door, then turned and looked at her. ''You have a lot in common with Gabe. He's gone through a tough time recently. His younger brother died before Gabe moved to Sherman. You know what Gabe's going through. He could use the support.''

Apprehension cut through her midsection. Normally she was eager to help out someone hurting. But she didn't want to relive any unpleasant memories—hers or anyone else's. Besides, what she'd seen of Gabe Randolph convinced her that he was more than capable of handling his own responsibilities and problems.

She struggled to keep dismay off her face. ''When is he moving in?''

''Today.'' He opened the door of his office for her. ''I called your Aunt Wallis and she said she'd prepare the extra bedroom.''

Dina barely stifled a groan. Now he'd gotten Aunt Wally, who had retired and was living at Dina's farm, involved, too. Her aunt had survived in a man's world for too long and knew how to get her own way. Once Aunt Wally set her mind on something, there was no arguing with her.

Dina couldn't fight both JD and Aunt Wally. It looked like she was now saddled with Gabe Randolph. She sighed. "Pretty sure of yourself, weren't you?"

"I knew you'd never turn away someone in need." JD gave her his first full smile, the Paxton charm very evident. "Besides, what other solution is there?"

She did need the help, at least temporarily. If Gabe Randolph turned out to be a problem, she would handle it herself. Today, she wanted to leave JD with a smile on his face. "I've got to get home."

She left the fire station twenty minutes later and hopped into her battered van, which was parked out front. The tired engine coughed and sputtered as she pulled away from the curb. It sounded as frustrated as she felt. She was twenty-eight but felt one hundred and eight.

Her pottery driver was two weeks late in delivering her order. The devastating fire last night had left another gaping black hole in Sherman's downtown and dropped a whole set of fears on the small community. Now she was going to play landlady to a man she didn't know and wasn't sure she wanted to know. For three years, she'd had a nice, peaceful life. What happened?

She turned into the narrow, tree-lined driveway and drove past the sagging, weatherworn shed and around the final bend.

An unfamiliar pickup truck was parked in front of her porch.

She pulled up next to the truck and cut the engine. Her hands tightened on the steering wheel as a long-legged man with waves of thick, dark brown hair swung down from the truck's cab.

Gabe Randolph sure hadn't wasted any time getting here.

Dina took a close look at the man who was going to be living in her house for the next couple of months. Well over six feet tall, he looked as solid as granite and about as bendable, too. If a woman were truly gullible, she'd believe this man could arm wrestle fate and end up the victor. He certainly appeared to be more than capable of handling her pottery and any other thing that got in his way. It would be too easy to lean on a man like him.

She swung open the van door and met his gray eyes. "Hello, Mr. Randolph." There was something about Gabe Randolph that made her nervous whenever she was around him. He was always watching her—as if he expected her to make a misstep of some sort.

"Call me Gabe." The deep gruffness of his voice cast disturbing vibrations through her nerve endings.

Pulling her reluctant body from the sticky vinyl seat, she swung out of the van.

Standing on the ground, however, put her at a definite disadvantage. In the past, she'd found it easy to ignore the wolf whistles to her less-than-beautiful, but not-quite-homely features. But under Gabe Randolph's intense gaze, she felt her skin blush and break out into an unladylike sweat beneath her knit T-shirt and paint-splattered jeans. Her full breasts—which had developed when her girlfriends were still stuffing their bras with socks—felt heavy and tingly. Even with Jerry, she'd never been this conscious of her physical assets and deficiencies.

She didn't trust the feeling.

"You've recovered from the fire, I see," he commented.

She lifted her chin. "Yes, I did. Thank you for your assistance."

"Glad to help out."

She crossed her arms over her chest protectively. "Exactly what were you doing so close to the feed store during the fire?"

He shrugged his powerful shoulders. "The other fire fighters were trying to reach you from the front and back. You came out a side door. I happened to be in the right place at the right time."

She registered his bland, unsmiling expression and decided they'd both prefer to put last night to rest. She dropped her arms and squared her shoulders. "I don't know what JD told you, but I can't afford to pay you very much."

"I don't expect to be paid. I just appreciate exchanging a little muscle for room and board."

She gave a brisk nod. "This is my busy season for the pottery and I don't entertain much."

Humor flickered for a moment in the gray depths of his all-seeing eyes, but his tone contained an agreeable edge. "If you're worried about your privacy, I'm usually working from late morning till midnight at the restaurant. I should be able to stay out of your way."

She cleared her throat and tried to cast away her doubts. Her dislike of him seemed irrational and almost petty, which was totally unlike her. She usually responded to people on a very warm and compassionate level. She owed Gabe the same courtesy—after all, he had saved her life. "I guess it's settled then."

"You don't mind if I move in today, do you?" Gabe gestured behind him to the belongings packed into the back of his pickup. In the process, his shirt gaped open, and Dina caught a glimpse of the naked, powerful chest inside his shirt. Her heartbeat jitterbugged.

"Today would be fine," she finally said before she abruptly spun around and walked toward the house.

How in the heck was she going to survive the next few weeks? Those hard, probing eyes and that glimpse of his chest sent curlicues of heat spiraling through her. The farm was relatively large. It wasn't as if they'd be stumbling over each other. So why did she suddenly fear a hot cinder had landed in her yard, and she wouldn't have any better success at putting out this fire than the last?

Dina Paxton was an enigma, Gabe decided three hours later, after he'd moved his belongings into the house and had helped unload pottery bowls from the semitrailer, which had dumped its load and left an hour ago. Dina had made it clear where she wanted the pottery bowls arranged inside the paint-chipped, ragged-looking shed, and then she'd gone silently about her business of stacking the smaller crocks.

The woman definitely wasn't pleased about his presence in her domain. That didn't matter. She had nothing to fear.

Gabe was looking for peace and quiet far away from the hysteria gripping the town. Two devastating fires in six months—in a town where the folks were still reminiscing about the huge granary fire in '48—were making people jittery and understandably short-tempered.

He had to admit that he'd been surprised, however, when he drove into Dina's farmyard. The big house and its surroundings were lush with the character and charm of Mother Nature. The farm was a place similar to what he had in mind when he thought of a home for himself someday. The colonial-style house was well built and appeared large enough to hold his whole family and then some. It made him wonder why Dina didn't have a family of her own to fill it.

He knew JD's daughter-in-law had been widowed for several years. He also knew she hadn't dated or shown any inclination of settling down to marriage again. She was a well-off woman who could attract any flesh-and-blood male if she made the effort.

Although she wasn't drop-dead gorgeous, Gabe considered her comfortably attractive. She was pleasing to the eye, but didn't have the come-hither looks that could drive a man crazy with jealousy if another man came within eye range. Tall and leggy in faded jeans, she filled out her clothes nicely. He figured she was also just the right height so that a man wouldn't have to throw his back out to kiss her.

Gabe wondered what Dina would do if she guessed his lusting thoughts. Run for those hills behind the house, probably. She'd made it clear months ago when she first met him that she didn't want to get too friendly. Ironically, that wary reaction had caught his attention immediately.

When he had arrived in Sherman, his bachelor status hadn't gone unnoticed by the community's single females. Bachelors were a prime commodity in the small town, and he'd been inundated with tempting chocolate chip cookies, mile-high cakes and rich brownies accompanied by the inevitable I'm-available invitations. Sweets had never been his weakness, and he was a man who liked to do his own hunting.

But Dina Paxton wasn't tempting bounty in his book, either.

When JD introduced him to Dina, Gabe noticed both the snapping intelligence in her green eyes and her lack of coy artifice. Cinnamon and spice. A potent combination.

Her response to him had been almost frigid, however.

At first he was amused by her lukewarm response. She, with the great smile and legendary compassion, had a kind word for everyone—everyone except him. That suited him just fine. He didn't intend to get involved with the town's guardian angel who put everyone else's safety ahead of her own. He knew from personal experience that do-gooders on a mission couldn't be stopped no matter what anyone else said. If she wanted to put her own neck on the line, he wasn't going to get in her way.

So what was he doing here?

He was here because he was a damn fool.

When he'd seen Dina struggling to elude the fire's clawing grasp the night before, he'd charged past the zone of safety to pull her from harm's way. Dina's eyes had opened. "Thank you" was all she said, but it was enough for him to see past the armor she usually wrapped around herself and catch a glimpse of the sensitive, vulnerable woman inside. In that moment, his protective instincts surged to life. He had been drawn into their depths and her pain, in spite of himself.

Later, when JD suggested Gabe move to temporary quarters at Dina's farm, Gabe ignored his inner voice of common sense and agreed.

Now, with the crocks carefully lined up against the wall, Gabe followed Dina out of the shed. One-quart crocks covered the flatbed, waiting to be moved to the workshop at the back of the house. The rest of the pottery sat on neat pallets inside the shed.

He wiped the sweat dripping down his temples and filled his lungs with the crisp, late-October air. His gaze swept the lofty evergreen-covered hills and then settled back on the woman who watched him from a short distance away.

At this moment, she appeared in harmony with her environment, her red hair highlighted by the sun's beams. It was difficult to remember that only the night before she'd been in a race with Death and had nearly lost. She looked very much alive this morning and startlingly beautiful.

For his own sanity, he forced his gaze away from her. "I'm surprised you can hear Sherman's fire whistle out here."

"I don't," she answered. "The county dispatcher notifies me through a voice pager. The fire department is only a few miles down the road, and I can be there within minutes."

"You've lived here long?"

For a moment, her remoteness faded as her face softened. "My grandfather and father grew up here. I can't imagine living anywhere else."

Gabe stared off into the distance at the tall, imposing bluffs across the river. The marks made by the passing centuries scarred the faces of the rocks. At the foot of those ageless monuments meandered Old Man River. There was a sense of stability and peace to this place. A man could grow content. So could a woman. He wondered why Dina volunteered for the multitude of projects in town that took her away from all this. He'd seen her dashing from a volunteer fire fighters' meeting yesterday to a playground meeting at the park. He'd heard all about the heated discussion between Dina and the mayor's wife over what brand of equipment was safer. It was no surprise to anyone that Dina won the argument. Then last night, she'd been back in town battling the fire. The woman seemed to have a guardian angel complex.

"I'm surprised you leave this serenity to fight fires." His voice sounded judgmental even to his own ears.

The warming on her face suddenly disappeared. "Somebody has to volunteer." She turned her back on him. "I have to get ready for a church meeting. There's also a carnival at the school so I won't be home until late. Don't worry about the pottery today. You can bring up the crocks to my workroom tomorrow.'' With that, she spun around and walked at a brisk pace up the lane.

Gabe stood still and watched her walk away. He wondered what had raised the ice wall. She'd just started to thaw a bit when he'd asked her what should have been an innocuous question about her reasons for being a fire fighter, then the icicles had formed again.

Was the fire fighting a hobby or did she have an unhealthy attachment for saving the world as his brother, Danny, had?

Danny's zealous quest hadn't been deterred by common sense or the love of his family, and Dina Paxton seemed no different, Gabe told himself. She thought she could change the world and not get burned.

If he was smart, he'd pack up his truck and go back to town. He'd probably be more comfortable pitching a tent in the state park than living with a bloody saint. But he couldn't forget the raw need he'd seen in Dina's eyes or the fragile warmth of her body after he'd pulled her from the fire. He'd seen the softness and the compassion.

By nature, he was both fiercely protective of those he cared for and very determined to succeed at anything he set his mind to. He was drawn to Dina in a way he didn't understand and would do best to ignore.

He'd learned the hard way that his protectiveness could drive someone away.

But the memory of Dina's vulnerable green eyes haunted him, preying on his old fears.

He *should* obey the lady's no-trespassing signs and go about his business. So why did he have a gut feeling he was about to do something stupid?

Chapter Two

Dina walked through the kitchen doorway the next morning and ran smack-dab into a flannel-covered chest.

"Good morning," Gabe's deep voice rumbled in her ear. Big warm hands clasped her arms and steadied her weaving body.

With her head pounding from lack of sleep, she peered through her blurry eyes into his brooding gray gaze. Was there no justice in the world? When she'd agreed to this living arrangement, she hadn't considered a big, musky-scented male would be loitering in her kitchen first thing in the morning.

She wedged her hands between them and pushed away from a body too warm to be normal. "Excuse me."

"Do you always walk in your sleep?" His growl sounded as disapproving as ever.

She narrowed her gaze, trying to clear her foggy brain. "Do you always take up the whole doorway?" she snapped.

"Sorry, I didn't realize I'd crossed the centerline." The corner of his mouth lifted in cynical amusement. "Slow riser?"

"Only on my good mornings." She groaned, trying to keep back a flush. She sounded like an absolute idiot. His steady regard made her nervous and uncharacteristically chatty. "Actually, I had a late meeting with the mayor and the town planning committee last night. It went into the wee hours of the morning."

He seemed to take an unusual interest in the dark circles under her eyes. An enigmatic expression had replaced his usual disapproving scowl, making her extremely self-conscious about the snug fit of her oldest pair of jeans and the deep V of her faded, paint-splattered shirt. Was she going to have to get all gussied up from now on, just so she could go into her own kitchen?

He broke the heavy silence. "How do you like your eggs?"

"Eggs?" She frowned. His conversation transitions were moving faster than her brain waves this morning. "We don't have any eggs. Or at least we didn't have any last night."

"I took the liberty of checking out your refrigerator before I left for the restaurant last night. There wasn't much in there that appeared to be edible. I brought home a few things," he told her.

She rarely opened a cookbook. Cold cuts, peanut butter and an occasional TV dinner were standard fare unless Aunt Wally experimented in the kitchen. And something definitely smelled better than Aunt Wally's tofu something-or-other. She walked over to the stove and peered into the frying pan. Yes, those were eggs, and there was bacon, too. She must have died and gone to Heaven.

But Heaven would have been kinder to her if they'd sent an uglier cook, Dina decided as Gabe brushed her arm to reach for a spatula.

"Did you know your toaster burns the bread?" he said.

"Adding lots of jelly takes the edge off the burnt taste," she replied absently.

A man's man like Gabe Randolph should have looked ridiculous standing in front of the stove. Instead, he appeared natural and at ease. His big hands handled the spatula with steady sureness. Would they be equally as steady on a woman's skin? she wondered. A delicious feeling spread through her as a flush rose to her face. *Where had that thought come from?*

The kitchen door suddenly swung open.

Aunt Wally walked into the room, dressed in stylish pants and a long vest, carrying her trusty camera. Her eyes widened appreciatively when she spotted the eggs Gabe was cooking. "Oh great, you can cook." She turned and gave Dina a meaningful look. "He can cook."

"I noticed," Dina responded dryly. She and her aunt had often joked about ordering a cook. Somehow, Dina hadn't expected the joke to evolve into a six-foot, very male reality, however.

Wally gave Gabe an approving grin. "Neither of us cooks very well. Not in the genes, I guess. Dina tried to make baked Alaska once."

Gabe cocked an eyebrow at Dina. "Baked Alaska? I'm impressed."

"Don't be," Dina warned. "It looked and tasted like fried Siberia."

It appeared a new job had just been added to his handyman duties. He didn't mind. Cooking always relaxed him. Besides, a man had to eat, and Gabe knew his meat-and-potatoes stomach couldn't digest "fried Siberia."

Wally grabbed her camera bag from a cupboard next to the back door. "I'm going into town to take some more pictures of the fire scene. By the way, Dina, Ralph Simpson called and said his dog is feeling better today."

"Good," Dina said, nodding. "I promised I'd stop by and give Hulk a new bone."

Wally snorted. "I doubt if that cranky old dog has any teeth left to chew with. You should have let him go to doggy heaven. It would have been a blessing."

Dina merely shook her head. "Don't let Ralph hear you say that. He dotes on Hulk."

Wally gave a final salute with her hand before she left the house.

"Your aunt doesn't like dogs?" Gabe asked.

Dina grimaced. "She likes dogs. She just doesn't think it's my job to rescue them." She rose from her chair and walked to the sink.

Gabe's gaze followed the gentle sway of her hips. He liked her tousled and fresh from sleep before she had a chance to raise any of those icy barriers. He much preferred this Dina to the cool one he had encountered yesterday. Was it only through daring fire rescues and treating her to breakfast that the true Dina emerged?

As she leaned over to fill a glass with water, he stopped chewing and silently admired the way her jeans hugged her shapely rear end. He couldn't help but notice how well she filled out her jeans. When she tipped back her head to drink, his eyes strayed to the creamy whiteness of her arched neck and throat. His gaze slipped downward, and his breath jammed in his throat as her shirt strained, revealing the peaks of ripe breasts that would fit perfectly into a man's palms.

He forced himself to swallow the food in his mouth and tried to recall what they were talking about. "What do you think your job is?"

"To do whatever it takes to keep everyone and everything safe in this town" was the answer.

"And your aunt has a problem with that?"

She rinsed her plate and shoved it into the dishwasher. "Aunt Wally has decided my fire fighting and other activities are standing in the way of my getting married again and having a family." She sighed. "I'm not sure why Aunt Wally believes I should settle into the family routine when she herself has never married."

"Perhaps she feels she missed something important."

Dina's laughter filled the room. Free and unrestrained. "You don't know Aunt Wally. My aunt gives new meaning to the word 'independent.' She's spent her life happily traveling the world as a free-lance photographer. A family or a husband would have smothered her." She stopped, then turned toward Gabe with a concerned frown on her face. "Maybe Aunt Wally's having trouble adjusting to retirement. She's writing a series of travel books and free-lancing for the local newspaper, but the change of pace is probably not what she's used to.''

From what Gabe observed of Wally Cassidy, he doubted that she was either bored or disenchanted with retirement. "Maybe your aunt's just worried about you."

Dina shook her head slowly. "If you're talking about what happened at the fire, my aunt knows I am a well-trained fire fighter and I never take foolish chances."

He draped his arms across his chest and considered her through narrowed eyes. Did she think she was invincible or did she just not care that she'd probably scared her aunt witless? "So while you're watching over the entire community, who's watching your backside?"

Surprise blanketed her expression. But within seconds, she got herself under control as the emotional shutters— which he was beginning to recognize and despise—dropped into place. "In case you're worried, you won't have to rescue me again," she said with coolness. "I'm used to taking care of myself."

Common sense warned him to back off. "I'll keep that in mind."

She gave him a leery look as if she wasn't sure whether to believe him or not. Finally, she shrugged her shoulders and started toward the door. "I need to get to work."

Gabe stared at the door that swung shut behind her and stroked the hard edge of his jaw. The lady was not as invincible as she would like to believe. Her dance with Fate the night before had been too close for comfort. Sherman was a small community, and yet they'd had two explosive fires within the past six months. Fortunately, nobody had been killed. But Gabe couldn't quite dispel the knot of fear when he thought about what might have happened. What could *still* happen if another fire of that magnitude ripped down another building. Her aunt wasn't the only one who didn't like Dina's frontline proximity. He didn't like it, either.

And the fact that he didn't like it made him even more frustrated.

Dina retreated to her sanctuary with relief.

She'd staked her claim on this small one-room building

behind the house after Jerry died. After painting the walls a friendly bright yellow, she'd converted the room into a workshop where she'd started a business of painting on rustic stoneware crocks. Each finished crock she placed on the floor-to-ceiling shelves had given her a sense of accomplishment and provided her life with meaning. She had desperately needed that sanity then.

She sought peace now.

Ever since Jerry had died, she'd kept a tight rein over her life. Each day was rather routine, and she knew what to expect. Her business was both challenging and rewarding, and she enjoyed contributing to the various committees in the community.

So why was she feeling uneasy all of a sudden? She could blame it on the near-fatal fire. Even the memory of how close she'd come to meeting her Maker gave her the shivers. It was no wonder JD had reacted so strongly. She'd scared him, and she vowed never to do that again.

Dina sighed and stared down at the surface of the crock she held in her hand without really seeing it. It wasn't JD's concerned countenance that appeared in her mind's eye. It was Gabe Randolph's grim face.

He'd been here less than twenty-four hours, and she couldn't quite seem to block him from her thoughts. There was no denying that as a man he was appealing in a rugged way. Most women probably found him attractive. But she'd been around attractive men before and hadn't felt this edgy.

It wasn't his manly attributes that made her tense and wary. It was the hard-edged determination. This was not a man who sat back and let life happen. He was a man of action, a man of purpose. He was a man who knew how to get what he wanted and wouldn't let anyone or anything stand in his way.

And then there were the shadows she'd sensed behind those deep gray eyes. Perhaps those were what worried her the most. Never had she witnessed such pain on a man's face than when he'd held her in his arms after the fire. JD had told her Gabe's brother had died. Whatever had happened, she doubted Gabe had accepted his brother's death readily or easily.

Unfortunately, she knew all about that type of battle. She had her own scars and she had no desire to share Gabe's. She shook off her gloomy thoughts. Donning her apron, she selected a clean paintbrush and took a steadying breath. She picked up a crock.

The door swung open. "Where do you want these?" The male voice violated her hideaway without an ounce of mercy.

The crock in her hand almost slipped off her lap. She grabbed it and swung around to face her intruder. Even standing in the doorway with one foot over the threshold, he seemed to take up half the room.

"I didn't mean to startle you," he said.

"You didn't." She refused to admit to him or herself how much he unnerved her. "My hands were just slippery."

Alarm shot through her as she spotted the towering pile of pottery in his arms.

"You shouldn't stack the crocks so high." She reached out to save her precious pottery, quickly unstacking the column of crocks.

He nodded his acknowledgment as he carefully set down the remaining pots and then straightened. Moving around the room, Gabe watched Dina reclaim her seat next to the long wood counter and pick up her brush. He scanned the room with interest.

He hadn't known what to expect when he'd first walked into the room. He had to admit that her contrasting job choices were original and interesting. "Fire fighter and pottery painter. You're a lady of talent and contrasts, aren't you?"

She arched an eyebrow at him. "What did you do before you bought the restaurant?"

He settled his shoulder against the door frame as he watched her. "I managed a family-owned quarry."

Even though she figured he'd probably done some kind of physically demanding work, his answer still caused her to blink. "Forgive me, but I don't see the common ground there, either."

He shrugged. "Both of us are stimulated by variety, it seems."

She shook her head as a half smile covered her lips. "I'd make a lousy restaurant owner. I hate to cook."

"I hate heights so I'd probably make a disastrous fire fighter," Gabe acknowledged. He couldn't help but notice Dina's attempt to deny they had anything in common.

He studied her inventory of painted crocks. A bold black loon adorned one crock. Fluffy kernels of popcorn dominated the exterior of another. The colors Dina had chosen were vivid and appealing to the eye. No wonder her business was thriving. A shelf of painted bowls sat against the opposite wall. He crossed the room to take a closer look.

"Do you market these crocks locally?" he asked.

She shook her head. "Not yet. For the time being, I sell to retailers in the bigger markets nearby."

His curiosity kept building. He wanted to understand all the layers of this complex woman. "How did you get started in this business?"

"I bought a couple of crocks at a flea market three years ago after my husband died. My grandfather suffered a stroke following the accident, and I needed to keep close to home. Anything physical would have disturbed Gramps, so I doodled with some paints I picked up at an art supply store."

She could talk about that devastating time now without tears gathering in her eyes. A glimmer of sadness still lingered as she remembered the pain of losing Jerry, and then the desperation of watching her grandfather gradually drift away. She'd had a family—small though it was—then they were gone.

Until then, she hadn't understood the deep pain loving someone could bring. She knew now. Losing love, and living with the guilt and emptiness afterward, had been the cruelest lesson she'd ever learned.

Dina shook off her melancholy and made her tone brisk. "Painting the crocks filled the long nighttime hours after they were both gone. Someone suggested I try retailing them to gift shops and specialty stores. A business was born.''

Gabe's mouth tightened as he set a crock with a sad-eyed moose carefully back on the shelf. He didn't like the thought of the pain and regrets Dina had experienced. Yet he admired the inner resources she'd acquired in order to step back into life again. "Is Wally your only family?"

She nodded. "My parents were killed in a car accident when I was two years old. I don't remember them at all. My dad's father raised me. Later on I married my childhood sweetheart. Jerry and I had five years together before he died.''

To look at Dina now—as she chewed her lip in concentration, her chin tilted at a stubborn angle and her hand steady while she painted her clever designs—a person would never suspect that she had been in a tug-of-war with Death since the day she was born. There was no bitterness on her attractive face. Merely acceptance.

A gutsy admiration overrode the sympathy building within Gabe. Dina hadn't had the big, nurturing family like his when times got tough. She'd had to rely on herself. He knew how devastating it had been to lose his brother. He knew how hard it was to get back into sync after one's foundation had been broadsided.

He cleared the huskiness from his throat. "Fate cracks a cruel whip."

She didn't deny it. "I have the farm, my friends and my memories."

"What caused your husband's death?"

She hesitated for a moment. Then she lifted her chin. "He died in a construction fire. A kerosene lamp accidentally tipped over, and Jerry was trapped inside. They couldn't get to him in time."

A hiss escaped Gabe's mouth as he absorbed the impact of the unexpected blow. Another puzzle piece fell into its slot. "I'm sorry. Were you a member of the fire department then?"

"No." She lifted her head into a defensive angle as if she resented the question.

Had she watched her husband die? Was that why she'd become a fire fighter? Was she saving her husband every time she battled terrifying flames? He felt her pain and understood her need to take action. "You're a survivor," he said.

Her wary gaze met his. Understanding formed a bridge neither had sought, but both shared. Her hands tightened around the crock. "Yes, I survived," she responded softly.

"Does time make it any easier?" Gabe realized he was asking very personal and revealing questions, but he couldn't force himself to pull back. Dina had firsthand experience in dealing with real pain—the pain of being left alive.

"Do you mean, do I ever get over wishing I were the one who died instead?" she asked.

"Yeah."

Some of the hostile tension eased from her face. "Eventually, the railing against the injustice lessens. But I never accepted his death. Never."

Her head lowered over the crock again. She'd shut a door in his face, and this time he didn't bother trying to break it down. The lady had been through enough. She'd earned her right to privacy.

He started for the door when something caught his eye. On the far side of the room sat a crock. It stood alone, looking rather plain. Then he realized the crock had been turned around. He reached for the bowl.

"Don't!" Dina's strained voice stopped him.

Gabe saw her pain before she dropped those damn shutters over her eyes. If he was any kind of a gentleman, he would have obeyed her plea, but he was fresh out of niceties. He tipped the piece of pottery toward him. Vicious slashes of orange, red and yellow sprawled across the shiny surface. Angry flames leaped at him. It was a taunting, victorious fire. He saw the rage and the pain. He knew without asking that no pattern had been used to design this crock. Raw emotion had been the guiding hand.

Gabe fought his basic instinct to grab Dina and comfort her for the misery that still haunted her. But he knew her

pain went deeper than a hug could cure. He forced himself
to stay on his side of the room. Finally he said, "Is there
anything else I can get for you?"

"No, I have everything I need." She enunciated every
word clearly and succinctly. There was no doubt she was
telling him more than he asked.

His mouth tightened. In a few words, she'd said it all.
She'd learned to survive on her own. She didn't need him or
anyone else.

That was the trouble with would-be saints.

Where in the hell was she? Gabe cursed to himself, two
night later, as he peered through Dina's living room windows at the empty farmyard. Nothing moved. He resumed
his pacing, vowing he wouldn't look out the window again.
After all, he wasn't Dina's keeper. But she sure as hell
needed one. One look at her calendar and her do-gooder
activities was enough to drive a man to drink. Today she had
led the local Brownie troop on a hike up the bluff, taken
Ralph Simpson's dog to the vet for a postfire checkup and
driven across the river to La Crosse, Wisconsin, to pick up
somebody's niece at the mall. Then shortly after midnight,
just when he'd returned home from closing the restaurant,
the dispatcher had paged Dina about a fire at Alice Withers's house. Dina had raced out without a backward glance.

Now it was almost 3:30 a.m.

He made three more treks across the same piece of carpet
before he returned to his post next to the window. This was
just plain asinine. He didn't need this kind of gut-wrenching
worry. But there was no way he could trot upstairs and go
to sleep. He was being drawn to Dina despite all of his resistance. She was more woman than any other woman he'd
ever met.

Dina, who had been robbed of almost every member of
her family, could have buried herself with her cold stoneware pots and ignored the needs and sufferings of everyone
else. Such an action on her part would have been easily un-
derstandable. Instead, she'd made the town her family and

become an invaluable part of the community. She was an incredibly strong woman with a soft heart.

That, from his experience, was a deadly combination.

Damn! Where was she?

Had a major fire broken out tonight? One with the same deadly intensity as the other two? Perhaps this one would claim a life. Dina could be...

He grabbed his jacket and started for the door. Just then, a set of headlights beamed through the windows. Relief swept through him as he recognized the familiar shape of the van, slipping into its parking spot beneath a giant tree. He dropped his jacket. As soon as she walked through the door, he snapped, "Where in the hell have you been?"

She stopped in surprise. "I didn't think you'd still be awake."

"I don't sleep much."

She didn't comment on his sleeplessness but kept a wary eye on him. "Do you want some hot chocolate?" she asked him.

"You don't have to make it on my account."

She gave him an uncertain look as if trying to gauge his mysterious mood. She made a decision and opened the kitchen door. "How about if I make it for both of us?"

He followed her into the kitchen. "How bad was the fire?"

"It was a false alarm. Alice Withers called the department after she smelled smoke coming from her kitchen. JD discovered a wooden spoon caught under the heating element in her dishwasher." She pulled down a couple of mugs and ripped open envelopes of instant chocolate mix. "I spent more time calming and fighting the panic of her neighbors than checking out Alice Withers's house. People are a shade nervous these days."

Aren't we all? "Any word yet on the cause of that fire the other night?"

"The preliminary investigation claims it was the work of an arsonist." She bit her lip and frowned as she set aside the spoon she'd been using. "But they don't have a suspect yet."

The false alarm tonight had practically created a riot. People were starting to look at their neighbors with open distrust.

It bothered her that no strangers had been spotted in town the week prior to the fire. The arsonist appeared to be very familiar with the habits of the town, and that kind of familiarity meant he had to have been seen.

Unfortunately, fretting about what happened didn't solve anything. She'd learned that much over the past three years. A day at a time had been her creed for living; she'd have to implement it now and hope for the best.

She stowed the mugs in the microwave. After she pushed a couple of buttons, she turned around and faced Gabe. She figured it was time to change the subject. "And what about you? What have you been fighting?"

A hood came down over his eyes. "What makes you think I've been fighting anything?"

Dina cocked her head and gave him a narrow-eyed gaze. Ever since she'd walked through the door, she'd wondered uneasily if the real fire tonight wasn't standing in the middle of her kitchen. There was a relentless energy radiating from Gabe. He looked like a man preparing to do battle. What had set him off? She hoped he didn't think that just because he'd rescued her from the fire the other night, she needed a bodyguard. She didn't need someone watching over her. He'd been here three days, and so far she'd managed to keep some distance between them. It appeared she wasn't going to be able to avoid him tonight, however.

"Maybe fighting isn't the right word," she said. "How about fencing with ghosts? Ghosts of memories. Ghosts of regrets. They all come out in the wee hours of the night."

"You're familiar with them?"

"We're old acquaintances." She handed him a steaming mug, leaned against the counter on the opposite side of the room and considered the brooding man across from her. What would it take to soothe the troubled lines from his face? She decided to take the bull by the horns. "JD told me that you lost your brother. How long has it been since he died?"

"Ten and a half months."

She saw the bleakness blanket his face. She remembered the emptiness all too well. "What happened?"

He took his time answering her. His jaw stiffened and then slowly relaxed. "Danny got caught in a gang war, and he was shot."

Dina's hand tightened around her mug. "He was a member of a gang?"

He shook his head slowly. "No, he was helping a homeless friend into a shelter on a cold night, and they accidentally got caught in the cross fire between two warring groups of kids."

"I'm sorry," she whispered. She didn't know what else to say. Now she understood his fury and helpless pain when he'd pulled her from the feed-store fire.

She recognized Gabe's ghosts. They were old buddies of hers. Futility. Anger. She'd been introduced to them long ago during many long and dark nights.

His pain battered at her defenses, slipping through the carefully constructed barriers. A need to comfort almost overwhelmed her. Identifying with Gabe was a dangerous emotion for her. It exposed her own vulnerability and bred a physical awareness she had previously safeguarded against. She knew she couldn't cross the line and get involved with Gabe. It put every ounce of control she'd mustered in jeopardy.

Gabe Randolph wasn't JD or Aunt Wally. She had to remember that and keep on guard. However, she couldn't ignore his suffering. It was too familiar, and try as she might, she felt an emotional link form between them. One that she instantly distrusted and feared because it was more than emotional. Something else came to life within her, as well.

Under the harsh glare of the kitchen light, she was suddenly conscious of Gabe as a man. Her kitchen seemed to shrink in size. Maybe the intense heat from the fire the other night had unbalanced her equilibrium.

She couldn't help but notice he had released the top two buttons of his shirt. There was an aura about him that shouted *male*, and her body answered *female*. Like thickening smoke, Gabe was seeping into every corner of the house and into her consciousness all too easily.

For her own sanity's sake, she needed to keep her distance. Her own ghosts still lingered. She understood them, respected them. She would be wise not to tangle with Gabe's, as well. A bond between them would be hazardous to her emotional well-being.

She thrust her mug into the sink, turned on the faucet and searched for a neutral conversation topic—something that would dispel the mounting tension and growing emotional currents charging through the kitchen. "Why did you move all the way to Sherman? Your hometown of Quarry City is several hours from here. Don't you have any other family?"

Thankfully, he stayed on his side of the kitchen. "I have another brother and a sister, plus my mom and dad. Add to that a sister-in-law, brother-in-law and several assorted offspring. Everyone else still lives in Quarry City. When my younger brother moved back home and took over the quarry, it was time for me to go out on my own."

She easily related to the need to be alone. "Each of us finds our own way to cope and heal."

He crossed the room and set his mug down next to hers. "Is that why you became a volunteer fire fighter?"

Dina stiffened. He was crowding her again, moving into spaces she considered private. The atmosphere in the room changed. Electrical currents darted between them as she recognized the aggression coming from him. He reminded her of an eagle circling the bluffs, searching for prey.

She could have refused to respond. Hiding wasn't her style, however. "I joined the fire department six months after my husband's death. I took every level of training possible, even the aircraft rescue course."

"I wasn't aware Sherman had a rescue plane."

She lifted her chin. "We don't. But I'll be prepared if we ever get one."

His gaze continued to draw hers into their gray depths. "Can anyone ever be completely prepared for life?"

She wrapped her arms tightly around her. "I have to try."

"You've chosen a dangerous path." His tone contained lethal softness.

She shook her head. "There are no safe paths."

The tightness of his jaw never relaxed. It seemed as if his expression became colder. "You're living in a fool's paradise."

Fury sparked and flamed within her. How dare he judge her! "Why? Because I wear a fire helmet? Because I saved an old dog? Or because I'm trying to make the world a safer place?" she retorted.

His fingers curled into fists. "Do you honestly think you can save the world and not get scarred? A kind heart is a victim in today's world."

"Maybe. But I don't have a death wish, and I can't turn my back on people in need." She inhaled a shaky breath, trying to keep the memories at a safe distance. But the regrets were only just below the surface. "Babies will be born and old people will die. That's life. But people like Jerry and your brother didn't deserve to die. Somebody has to fight for them and make sure others don't die like they did. Before their time."

"You can't control life," he said forcefully. "You'll only end up hurting yourself if you try."

His words pierced through the slim shield she wore over her heart. For a moment, she couldn't answer him. She tried to muster her convictions and keep her focus on the only course left open to her. Finally she found a whisper. "True hurt is when you live with the responsibility of someone else's death on your conscience."

What the hell did she mean about being responsible for someone else's death? Gabe wondered after Dina left the room. Did she suffer the same "what if" guilt he did? *What if* he'd been there—would Danny have died?

Dina should have slapped his face, Gabe admitted to himself. He'd deliberately baited her. He wasn't sure why he was so leery of Dina being a fire fighter. She looked more than capable of handling herself in a crisis situation. And she had been running *from* the fire, not into it. His fear seemed out of proportion to the facts.

He understood Dina's need to plunge into action after death slashed apart one's life. He'd experienced the same need following Danny's death. Danny was the younger brother who had followed Gabe everywhere during his growing-up years. There had been almost ten years difference between their ages, but they'd been close from the time Danny was a toddler and could tag along after Gabe. The distance between them only emerged as they grew older, and Danny became obsessed with helping others.

Right after Danny's graduation from high school, their father had suffered a heart attack. When Danny had wanted to leave Quarry City to pursue his own interests, Gabe had argued against it. Their other brother, Kyle, was almost ready to graduate from college and wouldn't be home for several months. Gabe had encouraged Danny to attend a nearby college so he could help out occasionally at the quarry, but Danny saw through his ploy to keep him under Gabe's protective wing. Danny wanted to move out into the world and make a difference. He left home with his high hopes and strong ideals paving the way for his future.

Gabe could clearly remember the day Danny left. His gut had been wrapped up in a knot. There was nobody on earth closer to a saint than Danny, but in Gabe's opinion that was what made his brother so vulnerable. Danny still had trouble remembering to look both ways when he crossed the street.

Then two years later, Gabe's worst fears were realized. Danny was dead.

At the funeral, Gabe had spoken to the many friends Danny had made since he'd left Quarry City. Over and over again, he heard how happy his brother had been. During his two years away from home, his baby brother had helped open two much-needed homeless shelters. It was a considerable accomplishment for a tender young man. Gabe's pain gradually eased.

But while he'd learned to accept Danny's career choice, he hadn't been able to accept his brother's untimely death.

After his brother, Kyle, took over the management of the quarry, Gabe took a couple of months off to travel the country. He'd needed to overcome his sense of anger and futility. Time and the love of his family had eventually been his healer.

During his journey home, he'd stopped in Sherman to visit his father's old friend, JD, and an empty building attracted his eye. Within months, he'd moved to Sherman and opened the restaurant. The challenge and ultimate success of running his own business had filled a certain void in his life and he was learning to be content.

Until he met Dina Paxton.

His brow furrowed into dissatisfaction.

He wished the lady could understand the risks she was taking. It was just as unacceptable for Dina to risk her life saving a dog as it was for Danny to die for a noble cause. His younger sibling had given so much to others and had lost his life in the process. Danny would never have a chance to marry or to have a child. The same thing could happen to Dina.

Gabe didn't consider himself a male chauvinist, but he recognized there was more to life than the work and civic responsibilities that dominated Dina's life.

She was a nurturer, taking care of everyone else. *But who took care of her when she had a problem?*

She was vulnerable—ignoring her own needs for the sake of others.

Just like Danny.

But whereas Danny had a family to come home to, Dina was a woman who had learned to handle her own fears and tears because there had been no one else to protect her.

In Gabe's mind, that was unacceptable.

Chapter Three

Nothing was going right today, Dina groaned to herself. It had been five days since the investigators had combed through the rubble, and JD had been unusually quiet about their findings. She'd come into town to see if she could pry an update from him about the ongoing fire investigation. He must know something. The hush-hush was making people as nervous as the fire did, and Dina wanted to know what the heck was going on. But JD hadn't been in his office.

"Dina."

Dina turned around and spotted her aunt crossing the street. She met Wally at the curb. "I didn't know you were coming into town today, Aunt Wally. I was just about to see if JD was at Lil's Coffee Shop. Do you want to join me?"

Wally, dressed in a formfitting jumpsuit and corduroy jacket, shook her head. "Lil's is closed. Let's head over to Gabe's restaurant instead. The morning crowd has moved over there until Lil gets her roof fixed."

Dina hadn't seen too much of Gabe since the night of the false alarm, although he'd made his presence known. His coat hung next to hers in the hall closet, the refrigerator was stocked full of food, and small chores she had postponed had been completed without fanfare. If he had been anyone else, she'd be delighted with the results of the arrangement. But Gabriel Randolph wasn't anyone else.

And if she was wise, she should continue to avoid Gabe. But she hadn't been inside Dare'n Gabe's Restaurant since it had opened, and her curiosity overrode her better judgment.

Entering the restaurant with Wally, she discovered an eclectic assortment of odds and ends tastefully decorating the cedar-lined walls. She wasn't sure exactly what she'd expected, but the pervading sense of comfort and warmth surprised and welcomed her.

"Hi, Dina and Wally." A middle-aged waitress with short graying hair waved to them. "There's an empty table over there if you'd like to sit down."

"Hello, Vivian. How's Frank doing?" Dina asked.

"He's doing much better. Thank you for giving him that crock. He was tickled to death." Vivian gave her a harried smile. "Excuse me, I'll be with you in a minute."

Wally stopped to talk to several of the other patrons while Dina moved through the maze of tables and chairs. She noticed Gabe working his way through the room greeting his customers. He looked like a man in control of his own environment. He played the part of host well.

Dressed in a casual denim shirt and fitted jeans, he looked entirely too appealing as he chuckled at something one of his customers said. The sound was a pleasurable rumble, rich and vibrant, drawing the attention of the other diners while warming the blood of every female—including her own.

Just then he looked up and met her gaze. Male satisfaction gleamed at her. Her hormones snapped to attention.

Get a grip. You came in here to look for JD. Not Gabe. Dina forced herself to give him a cool nod before she broke eye contact. She performed a visual search of the room. Unfortunately, her father-in-law didn't seem to be anywhere in sight. She sat down.

A stooped, gray-haired man shuffled up to her table. "Hi, Dina. I've been lookin' for you. I bought you a small gift from me and Hulk."

From across the room, Gabe watched Dina give the old man—whom he recognized as Ralph Simpson, the owner of the dog in the fire—a warm smile as she graciously accepted his present. A gaudy pumpkin pin emerged from the wrapping.

"How beautiful!" she said. "Thank you, Ralph. But you shouldn't have wasted your money on me."

The hard-of-hearing Ralph frowned in confusion, looking down at his stained plaid shirt. "I've got honey on me?"

"No, Ralph. Money! You shouldn't have spent your *money* on me!" she corrected patiently.

A light dawned on Ralph's face. "Okay, I'll send you money next time."

Dina's expression wavered between despair and humor. Gabe wasn't sure why she bothered with the old guy. Ralph Simpson had a chronic gambling problem and was a notorious flirt. Most of the people in town tried to avoid him whenever possible. But Dina didn't show a flick of impatience with the old geezer.

Ralph's spinster sister, Kordelia Simpson, marched up to the table and yanked on her brother's arm. "Come on, you old fool, quit your flirting."

Ralph refused to budge. Ignoring his sister, he pressed closer to Dina. "Did you happen to notice the newest Hollywood adventure flick has finally come to the movie house in La Crosse, Dina?"

"I sure did, Ralph. We'll need to make a date to go," she shouted into his ear.

As Ralph beamed and his sister glowered, Dina placed her hand on the older woman's arm. "You're welcome to come along, too, if you'd like, Kordelia."

Kordelia looked outraged at the suggestion. "I don't waste my money on such frivolous entertainment. And you shouldn't, either, Ralph."

"Kordelia, you prune-faced old bag, quit trying to run my life—" Ralph started to yell.

Gabe decided it wasn't good for business to have the Simpson siblings come to blows in the middle of his restaurant. He sauntered over to the table. "Ralph and Kordelia, do you need a table?"

Ralph turned and eyed Gabe suspiciously. "Do I know you?" he demanded.

"This is Gabe Randolph, the new owner of the restaurant," Dina answered. When Ralph's face looked blank, she raised her voice a little louder. "The owner of this place where you've come to eat."

"He's got no feet?" Ralph tried to peer around the table to where Gabe stood.

Kordelia yelled at him. "He owns the place where you eat! Next time wear your hearing aid, you deaf coot!"

"You don't have to shout, Kordelia. I'm not deaf." The affronted gentleman turned his back on their table. Moving slowly toward a booth in the back of the room, he muttered loudly, "He does too have feet."

As the quarreling twosome moved away, Dina frowned. "I wish Kordelia wouldn't yell at him like that. I know she hurts his feelings."

"Ralph's an old lech," Wally said as she sat down across from Dina. "The only reason he doesn't wear his hearing aid is so he has an excuse to peek down the front of your shirt. He doesn't have trouble hearing any of those movies you two go to, does he?"

"Of course not." Dina gave her aunt a mischievous glare. "He wears his hearing aid to the movies. And I always wear a high-necked blouse."

Wally snorted. "You wouldn't have to wear a high-necked blouse if you'd go on a date with a man who wasn't bald and wrinkled from old age." Wally turned to Gabe. "You don't have that problem, do you, Gabriel?"

"Don't have to wear a high-necked blouse or have to date bald, wrinkled old men?" he asked blandly.

Dina choked as the water in her mouth threatened to go down the wrong pipe. Gabe leaned over and thumped her on the back, his warm palm sending her body into further distress.

"Thanks, I'm fine now." She held up a restraining hand.

He was too close. His musky scent filled her head, and she tried to move away from his hand's range.

Gabe dropped his hand.

"How's business, Gabriel?" Wally asked.

"Business is good." Gabe pulled out a chair. His legs bumped Dina's, and he noticed with amusement that she kept her eyes deliberately trained away from his.

When she first came through the door, he couldn't deny the surge of energy flowing through him. He liked having her in his restaurant and sitting so deliciously close. Her informal attire of casual slacks and a turtlenecked shirt showcased her femininity. The soft pink knit of the shirt highlighted her creamy skin and gave her cheeks a soft blush. Her rolled-down collar offered a tantalizing view of her slender, graceful neck and the hollows below her ears. He wondered, not for the first time, how sensitive those enticing pockets would be to a man's lips. She'd no doubt taste like smooth honey.

Sitting this close to her was not a good idea, a voice in the back of his head warned. *Hell, so what's new,* he almost snorted aloud. The woman had been tormenting his sanity for days now. He'd tried to plan his schedule so he could keep a safe distance. The more he skirted her proximity, however, the more he was drawn.

She could have ignored the Ralph Simpsons of this town and created a small circle of close friends as most people did, but Dina made herself available to everyone. She not only went to the movies with Ralph, Gabe bet she probably enjoyed it.

Just then, Mayor Conrad and his wife, Essie Mae, stepped into the restaurant. The couple reminded Gabe of the fictional Jack Sprat who could eat no fat and whose wife could eat no lean. The mayor was a thin, short man who barely came to Gabe's chest, while Essie Mae—not taking into account the two inches added on to her poofed-up and repeatedly dyed blond hair—was at least six inches taller and outweighed her husband by a good hundred pounds.

The mayor walked over to talk to several patrons in the corner booth.

The mayor's wife, however, spotted them sitting in the middle of the room and made a beeline for their table, the flounces on her Southern-belle dress fluttering in her wake. Her eyes zeroed in on Dina. "Well, what do you have to say for yourself this time, young lady?"

Dina frowned. "I'm afraid you've lost me, Essie Mae. What subject am I supposed to address?"

"You know what I'm talking about," Essie Mae retorted in a loud voice designed to draw everyone's attention. "The fires. First the old machine shop and then the farm-and-feed store. You were the last person to visit the farm-and-feed store before it burned to the ground. Just like you were the last person in the old machine shop. Don't tell me that's merely coincidence."

Gabe saw Dina's lips tighten, but her voice was steady and even when she replied. "I wanted to buy it, not burn it, Essie Mae. I planned to open a craft store for area residents to sell their crafts or works of art on consignment. That store would have benefitted the entire community. Besides, I wasn't the only person in those buildings. The mayor was in there with me."

Essie Mae's tremendous chest heaved in indignation. "My husband owns that building. He had a right to be in there."

Wally scraped back her chair and gave Essie Mae a disgusted look. "I think you have a screw loose, Essie Mae. Why would Dina want to burn down those old buildings?"

Essie Mae sniffed. "Of course, you would defend her. She's your niece. Some of the rest of us aren't nearly so blind. The only thing those terrible fires had in common was that Dina had just been in the stores. Besides, who knows more about setting fires than a fire fighter?"

Gabe's gaze narrowed as a collective gasp resounded through the room at Essie Mae's accusation. How long had Essie Mae hated Dina? He knew the older woman liked to be the spokeswoman for the town. Somewhere along the way, she must have deemed Dina a threat to her status.

Dina felt a wave of resignation and fatigue flow through her. "I didn't have anything to do with those fires, Essie

Mae. Nobody hates fire worse than I do. Jerry died in a fire, or have you forgotten?''

Essie Mae's face twisted into a sneer. "How do we know you didn't start that fire and kill him, too? Maybe you're one of those pyromaniacs. Maybe you want to be a heroine so the entire town can worship at your feet."

Dina paled at the attack.

Vivian rose to Dina's defense as she shook her head vehemently, the lemonade pitcher jiggling precariously in the waitress's hand. "Oh, no, Dina's not that way. You know she's not."

A murmur of agreement whispered through the room.

"Bah! You all think Dina's so perfect, you can't see the truth." Essie Mae's face turned brittle.

Gabe kept his voice low and calm. "And what is the truth?"

Essie Mae turned her full attention on him, probably hoping she'd found a sympathetic ear in the midst of Dina's supporters. "If she'd married Billy Bob and had a few kids by now, she wouldn't be interfering with other people's lives and trying to run the town instead of settling down. She's put us all in danger."

"I don't see why marrying Billy Bob and having a family would put a stop to the fires." The steel in Dina's voice held a warning note.

Gabe frowned, wondering who Billy Bob was.

Wally leaned forward. "You can't lay this recent tragedy at my niece's doorstep. She has nothing to gain, whereas you and your husband could probably collect a nice little insurance nest egg. Just how much insurance do you plan to collect anyway? More than Dina offered to pay for those buildings, perhaps?"

"How dare you insinuate—"

Wally cut off Essie Mae's outrage. "Maybe the arsonist is someone with local connections. How about that no-good Billy Bob, Essie Mae? I've noticed he slinks into town quite frequently."

Essie Mae's face swelled to an ugly color. "Billy Bob left the day before the fire started!" she snapped. "He has no reason to terrorize us. That's absolutely preposterous."

"No more preposterous than Dina having anything to do with those fires," Wally retorted.

Gabe decided it was long past time for him to take charge of the deteriorating conversation. "Who's Billy Bob?" he asked.

Essie Mae gave him a dirty look. "Billy Bob's my nephew, of course."

"And he proposed to Dina?" He wanted to make sure he understood everything.

Essie Mae merely lifted her double chin.

Dina refused to meet his gaze.

Obviously no one wanted to pursue that line of questioning. He leaned back into his chair. "I'm sure JD will have something to report soon, and then everyone can rest easier."

"Humph." Essie Mae shot Dina one more nasty glare. "One can only hope our worthy fire chief and his investigators won't ignore all the evidence that's sitting right in front of their eyes."

Gabe noticed several of the customers' heads nodded in agreement. Unfortunately, Essie Mae had planted a nasty seed of suspicion.

He didn't for a moment believe Dina Paxton was guilty of anything, and he'd bet neither did the majority of the townsfolk. One only had to look at her clear green eyes to see the honesty and integrity directing every action she undertook. But the threat of more fires could destroy the community's collective common sense. He knew better than most that guardian angels were not immune to unwarranted attack and hurts.

This thought in mind, he decided this was one guardian angel who might need a little assistance.

Vivian moved forward with her lemonade pitcher. "Would you like some lemonade, Essie Mae?"

Gabe rose to his feet, his elbow bumping Vivian as she came abreast. The full pitcher of lemonade in the waitress's hand tipped over, and lemonade and ice cubes cascaded right into Essie Mae's face.

"Aaugh!" Essie Mae squealed as her hair sank like the *Titanic*. "You clumsy fool. How dare you!"

Dina watched with disbelief and then struggled to contain her amusement as black snakes of mascara slithered down Essie Mae's rouged cheeks.

The mayor, who had stayed conspicuously in the back of the room during his wife's attack against Dina, rushed forward. He tried plucking a lemon slice out of his wife's endless cleavage while she screeched like a chicken. Vivian alternated between patting Essie Mae's hand and trying to reinflate the punctured hairstyle.

Dina couldn't help but notice Gabe watching the comedic proceedings with a glint of satisfaction darkening his eyes. If she had any doubt that Gabe had staged this little drama, she had only to observe him calmly cleaning up the mess on the table and the floor or to see Aunt Wally's satisfied smile.

Essie Mae shoved aside her husband and glared at Gabe. "I'm going to sue you."

The mayor pushed his way between his wife and Gabe. "Now, Buttercup, it was an accident."

"Don't you Buttercup me! This man has humiliated me. I demand that we contact our attorney and—"

"That would be a shame, Essie Mae, because I wanted you to headline the style show for our first annual Christmas Party." Gabe's deep voice penetrated the First Lady's unladylike squawking.

"Bribery will get you—" Essie Mae stopped. Her face lightened. She attempted to fluff her sunken hair. "Style show? You want me to star in your style show?"

"If people knew you were the featured model, the party would be a success. We might even attract people from La Crosse and the Cities." Gabe's voice was smooth and beguiling.

Essie Mae sat up straight. Her chin lifted to a regal angle. "Well, I suppose we can overlook this tragedy. But if you're going to stay in business, I'd suggest you take a refresher course in grace and etiquette.'' She turned to her husband. "Come along, Bertrum. I'm beginning to feel chilled.''

Agitated chatter broke out among the restaurant patrons after the mayor and his wife left.

Gabe started circulating the room again and, a few minutes later, spotted Dina heading for the door. He handed Vivian the coffeepot. "Cover for me, Viv. I need to take care of some business.''

Dina wasn't going to escape without answering a few questions.

Gabe discovered Dina poking through the farm-and-feed-store ruins. Its one remaining blackened wall was perched perilously nearby. A knot of fear built in his gut. He didn't trust the crude bracing of boards reinforcing it.

"Dammit, lady! Are you trying to kill yourself?" He grabbed her arm and swung her around. He knew his fear was probably out of proportion and irrational, but the memory of pulling her from the burning feed store still hung fresh in his mind. "What in the hell are you trying to do? Have the rest of this rubble tumble down on top of you?''

Her icy green eyes glared at him as she tugged for him to release her arm. "I'm a fire fighter. I'm just trying to see if there are any clues that have been overlooked.''

"The ashes are cold. Poking around here isn't your job, is it?''

She wasn't winning the war to reclaim her arm and quit struggling for a moment. "I don't need a protector.''

"Could have fooled me." Gabe's gaze searched the burned-out shell in front of him. If there had been anything worth keeping in the building prior to the fire, it had now disintegrated into black soot. He'd be surprised if any clues could be found amid the charred layers. There was certainly nothing there worth Dina's jeopardizing her life. The ruthless inferno had been very thorough.

Dina scuffed her shoe against a small flat object at her feet, finally managing to dislodge Gabe's arm as she reached down to pick it up. "This looks like a dog tag. I wonder if it belonged to Ralph's dog. I just can't understand what that dog was doing here.''

Gabe had no interest in the wanderings of a worn-out dog. Now that he was assured Dina was in no immediate danger, he wanted to pursue his own questions. "Tell me about Billy Bob."

Dina pocketed the blackened object. "I grew up with Billy Bob, and he occasionally drops into town to visit."

"When did he propose to you?"

She shrugged as if receiving marriage proposals was an everyday occurrence. "He came out to the farm a couple of times last year. During one of his visits, he suggested I marry him so I wouldn't have to be alone." A glimmer of a smile crossed her lips as she remembered the strange proposal. "I don't think Billy Bob, who never seems to stay in one place very long, was as disappointed as Essie Mae when I turned him down." She rubbed the back of her neck.

"How disappointed was she?"

Dina looked exasperated. "If you think Essie Mae was mad enough to start all those fires, forget it. I'm not that good of a catch. Her little drama in the restaurant was probably a way to release some of her fear about the fires."

Gabe grunted. He wasn't convinced Essie Mae was just reacting to Dina out of fear. Essie Mae's attack seemed too personal. He knew he wasn't going to change Dina's view of Essie Mae, however, and decided to press on to the next issue. "What about your connection to those buildings that burned?"

She shrugged. "Essie Mae was grasping at straws. There couldn't be a connection. The mayor owns both buildings and several others along the downtown strip. It's a mere coincidence that both of the stores I expressed an interest in buying were burned to the ground."

"How many people knew about your interest?"

She gave him a sideways glance. "This is a small town. What's a secret one day is printed in the headlines the next."

"So everybody knew."

She frowned at his interrogative tone. "I can't believe my small business could elicit that much emotion. It doesn't make any sense. A lot of people would benefit from the craft store because I plan to offer consignment space to local craftsmen.''

Something just didn't feel right. He thought Essie Mae was right on target when she insinuated the coincidences were too unbelievable. ''Are you a threat to anyone?''

''I don't have any enemies in Sherman.'' Her mouth tipped with wryness.

Gabe's jaw firmed. How did one protect a woman who saw herself only as a rescuer and not as a rescuee? ''You could be the target. If everyone in this town knows everyone else and their business, it only stands to reason that they would know you might try to rescue a poor dog from a burning building.''

''That's ridiculous,'' she protested.

His fingers curled into a fist of frustration. ''Is it?''

She shook her head almost violently. ''This is my home. I've known everyone here from the time I was born—except for you. Maybe you're the one I should be looking out for.''

She started to step away from Gabe. All of sudden the ground seemed to shift. The wall wavered. *Crack. Rumble.*

''Get back!'' Gabe grabbed Dina and threw her down to the ground. Before she could protest, he dropped down on top of her to shelter her from the falling debris. Dina covered her head as Gabe curled protectively over her.

Whoosh! Ashes and soot flew through the air.

Then all was quiet. Neither one of them moved. Their pounding hearts beat in unison. Dina clutched Gabe's shoulders, trying to still the shivering suddenly tormenting her. For a moment it was enough to know they both were alive and breathing. She couldn't believe what had happened.

The last remaining wall had collapsed. If Gabe hadn't pulled her...

A rush of feet sounded. ''Are you two all right?''

Gabe searched Dina's face to make sure she was in one piece. Except for the pale face and a stiff expression of fear, she looked okay. If only he could quiet his stampeding pulse and vanquish the gut-wrenching fear.

What in the heck was going on? That damn wall shouldn't have fallen. JD would never have left the wall standing if there had been any danger. Gabe would stake his life on that.

He rolled to his feet and reached down to help Dina to hers as his eyes scanned the nearby area. People rushed toward them. It was mass confusion. He couldn't tell if anyone was acting strange or not. Everybody was upset.

"Are you two all right?" Wally came forward and hugged Dina. After they both nodded, she asked, "What happened?"

"I don't know," Gabe said. He looked down at Dina, who was shakily brushing the soot from her clothes. He wanted some answers himself. "Did you see anything? Anything different? Was there someone standing next to the wall?"

A sliver of vulnerability slipped across her face. Her body was stiff with shock...and denial. "Everything went so fast. I don't understand. The partition seemed fine just a few minutes ago."

He spun around, checking behind him to see if anyone was running away, but the thickening crowd blocked his view. "Did anyone see anything?"

The crowd didn't appear to hear him. They continued to press closer, their talking and shouting making it difficult to make sense of what everybody was saying. Wally had stepped back and was snapping pictures of the scene with her ever-present camera.

Gabe managed to wedge his way through the crowd, dragging Dina with him. His gaze raked the surrounding area, trying to pinpoint anything out of the ordinary. The ashes looked as black as ever. The boards that had braced the wall lay scattered around coal-colored debris.

He reached down and examined the boards for cracks or breaks. There were none. Someone had knocked over the wall. But why? Why would anyone want to hurt them or kill them?

The mayor pushed his way through the mass of people. "Do either of you need a doctor?"

"No, we're fine." Dina's wobbly assurance grabbed Gabe's attention.

She looked as if she was ready to collapse at any second. He had to get her out of here. He'd come back later and take a closer look at the ruins. "Come on, I'll drive you home. We can pick up your van later."

She wiped a smudge of dirt from her face and shook her head. "No. I'm fine."

Gabe didn't believe it for a moment. He lowered his voice so that no one else could hear him. "Dina, you shouldn't be alone. At least take Wally with you."

She refused to meet his eyes. "Aunt Wally will want to stay in town and develop pictures of this for the newspaper. I can drive myself."

"Dina—"

Her gaze flew up to meet his. "Look, I don't need you. It was an accident," she almost shouted. "I don't need a damn protector."

"Lady, you don't have a choice" was Gabe's savage reply.

Dina yanked her arm from his grasp and spun away from him. The noisy crowd moved between them, and she was severed from his sight before he could react.

He wanted to push them all aside and tug Dina back into his arms. That was the only way he'd feel she was safe. But he knew she only had a thin rein over her emotions. She wouldn't appreciate his protectiveness if she suddenly broke down in front of the entire town. And she'd have no compunction about throwing him out of her house if he tried something stupid. After what had happened, he couldn't risk that. There was no way he'd leave her now. The woman needed someone to keep an eye on her, and whether she liked it or not, he was the person.

The sand had just emptied to the bottom of the hourglass. Something was going on. That wall had been standing for a week since the fire. What made it collapse now? The common denominator in everything that had happened recently was Dina. Someone knew Dina was crawling through the rubble and had pushed the wall toward her.

Gabe curled and uncurled his fist. Unfortunately, Dina didn't seem to have any concept of the danger she was in. She appeared to be in full denial, but he couldn't afford the luxury of giving her the space or the time to get used to his presence.

That wouldn't stop him. He could no more stop being protective than Dina could stop trying to save a helpless dog. He wasn't even going to try. If he'd ever hoped to walk away from Dina before this thing was over, those hopes were now ashes. He intended to become her shadow until the danger had passed.

And then he would walk away. Lord knew, he didn't need a stubborn woman tormenting him for the rest of his life.

He pivoted and headed toward the fire station.

"Dammit, JD! When is this going to stop?" Gabe slammed his fist on the fire chief's desk thirty minutes later. JD had arrived on the scene immediately following Dina's departure and had helped clear away the crowd so his investigators could work. "Surely you've got some clue as to who is behind those fires."

Now JD tiredly sat in his chair, his chin resting on his steepled fingers, watching Gabe prowl. He shook his head. "We're working on it. All we know for sure is that both fires were started by an unidentifiable mixture of chemicals."

"That's all you have?" Gabe growled.

"You know I can't tell you all the details of the official findings. I've already told you more than I should have. You know more than most—more than Dina."

JD had confided in Gabe that there were certain similarities between the Sherman fires and other fires that had broken out during the past eighteen months in nine other states. All the fires had been started in abandoned buildings after midnight. All had been the result of an explosive combination of chemicals. With the exception of Sherman, all the fires had been set in major metropolitan areas. So far, little progress had been made in determining the identity of the perpetrator despite the number of investigators working on the cases.

None of it made any sense. What was the connection? Why would an arsonist pick this small town? And why did Dina seem to be the lightning rod drawing the strikes?

He lifted his shoulders, trying to ease the tension from his neck. Adding to JD's problems wasn't his intention, but neither could he ignore the increasing danger. "That wall shouldn't have toppled. The bracing didn't snap. Not a single board was broken." He planted his fists on the desk. He stared hard at the older man. "Why is Dina a target?"

"I don't know." JD didn't deny his assumption.

By the expression on the older man's face, Gabe suspected JD knew more than he was telling. "What aren't you telling me?"

JD gave him a troubled look. "I'm telling you everything I can."

Gabe's mouth tightened. "That's not good enough! She's your daughter-in-law! Or don't you care whether she lives or dies?"

JD rose from his chair and glared at Gabe, a spark of fury in the older man's eyes leaping to life. "Watch your mouth, son. If I wasn't worried sick about Dina, you wouldn't be living at the farm."

A light dawned. Grudging respect built within Gabe. He'd wondered at the time if JD had an ulterior motive for setting up the living arrangements at Dina's farm. "Why didn't you tell me you were worried about Dina?"

JD turned away from the desk and jammed his hands into his pockets. "At first, I wasn't sure she was in danger. There's still no conclusive proof she is, but I couldn't risk leaving her unprotected."

Gabe scowled. "Why didn't you tell me the truth?"

"Would you have moved out to the farm if I'd told you?"

Gabe didn't think it was necessary to answer the obvious. Besides, it was too late to change the facts as they now existed. "She wouldn't thank you for giving her a protector."

A cynical smile lit JD's expression. "Yeah, ain't that the truth? It runs in the family. Those Cassidy women are as stubborn as they come."

The two men shared a long look.

Finally Gabe said, "You're not giving me much to work with."

JD sighed as he followed Gabe to the door. "Dina needs you whether she wants to admit it or not. That's all I can tell you. I'll worry about the arsonist. You watch over Dina."

Gabe stared at his father's old friend. "Short of tying Dina to a bed, how am I supposed to do that?"

"That's one option, I reckon." JD's eyes twinkled. "I'll let you work out the details."

From his window, JD watched Gabe stride down the street. The door leading into the fire station quietly opened.

JD didn't move from his post as he felt the woman's presence steal up behind him. He frowned. "Maybe we shouldn't have interfered. This whole thing could backfire in our faces."

Her arms crept around his neck. "It's too late now. We'll just have to wait and see how it turns out."

JD turned around and gathered the woman in his arms. Had they done the right thing? He hoped she was right. What he wouldn't give for a crystal ball right now.

The woman moved into the light, but no one saw her. They looked past her as always. Their blindness made her burn with rage. How dare they patronize her and give her only a few crumbs of much-deserved respect? She had the power to bring them all to their knees, and they still didn't see the obvious.

Only she could save them, and no one else recognized it. They mocked her. Ignored her as if she didn't exist.

And it was all Dina Paxton's fault.

She was weak and obviously stupid.

She'd even saved the damn dog. And for what purpose? So the mutt could bark all hours of the night?

The dog should have died.

Darling Dina shouldn't have interfered. She was no savior. She had no real powers.

The wall should have finished her off.

Her phony pureness was nauseating. Did she think people didn't know she was shacking up with that new restaurant owner? The girl was a tramp. She led good men astray.

Even now, as everybody moaned and wrung their hands in worry over poor little Dina, they refused to understand the little tramp was the cause of all their misery. Poor little Dina! Bah! It wasn't fair.

The town must suffer another lesson. They needed to know who was in charge.

Late in the night, Dina stared at the ceiling. Her mind and body refused to relax as her memory replayed the scene earlier that day.

The near catastrophe had been too close. What had made the wall collapse? She'd tested its steadiness with the weight of her hand before she'd started her investigating. The wall hadn't budged. Something or someone had to have applied a lot of force to send the charred partition toppling.

She squeezed her eyes closed, recalling how she'd verged on hysteria. If Gabe hadn't been holding her, she'd have turned into a screaming ninny.

Her mind churned with confusing images.

She couldn't be in danger. She refused to believe that she was the arsonist's target. No unexplained accidents had occurred at the farm. The people truly in danger were the townspeople living along the two-block stretch of Main Street. Even Gabe was in more danger than she. The restaurant covered half a block and provided a big target. That building, too, had been empty for almost a year before Gabe had bought it. Perhaps the arsonist would go after it next. Maybe someone had been trying to kill Gabe instead of her.

Her stomach clenched at the thought.

She could still feel the strength and power of Gabe's arms as he protected her from the falling wall. The aftermath had been almost as devastating as the near-death experience itself. She'd wanted to cling to his strong arms and never let go. She'd never felt so out of control in her life, and she'd wanted to hand over all her hard-earned sanity to Gabe—a man she barely knew.

Why Gabe? Picturing every hard angle and crevice of his face stirred emotions she'd buried or never realized she had. Why did she react so differently to him than to everyone else she knew? Why did he spark feelings so unlike those she'd had for Jerry?

Jerry had been her buddy, her date to the high school prom and her one and only lover. She'd grown up with Jerry. Their relationship had matured from a lifelong friendship. There had been the anticipation and tingling excitement from the first kiss and the apprehensions when she'd first slipped beneath the covers with him on their wedding night. But she didn't ever recall the raw excitement she felt every time Gabe entered the room. Or the contentment of knowing he was near. She didn't recall both admiring and fearing Jerry's strengths at the same time. Not as she did with Gabe.

Was it because Jerry had helped patch up her scraped knees during her tomboy years? Or because they'd skinny-dipped in the pond together before they'd learned their bodies should be considered private and mysterious?

Was that why she'd never experienced this combustible "I am woman, you are man" feeling?

Her feelings for Gabe were strange and unwanted. Why couldn't she treat Gabe Randolph impersonally? He made her yearn for things she hadn't thought about in years. Traditional things. Things she'd never mastered when she was married. She'd tried to be a good wife to Jerry. She just never quite got the hang of it.

She wished her mother was alive and could counsel her. Give her guidance.

She tossed back the covers, suddenly very hot and utterly confused. Darn Gabe Randolph! Why was she wishing for the moon?

He wants to protect you!

Dina pulled her pillow over her head. *Stop it!* She didn't need a protector, a husband or a lover. She'd always been strong. Self-reliant. She'd had to be.

What power did Gabe possess that drew out the vulnerability she'd kept carefully hidden? Why did she fear for Gabe's safety more than her own? She'd never worried about Jerry, but then she hadn't believed Jerry would die. Jerry had always been so cautious. He shouldn't have died— he wouldn't have died if she hadn't let him down!

She thought she'd banished the guilt—her secret shame.

Gabe was stirring up more than just a few hormones.

For her own peace of mind, she had to stay clear of Gabriel Randolph.

Chapter Four

A week later, Gabe drove back to the farm after spending the afternoon working on his accounts at the restaurant. He'd stopped at the grocery store before heading out on the scenic highway. Since it was Sunday night and the restaurant was closed, he planned to fix dinner for Wally and Dina. He considered it a celebration dinner—celebrating the peace and stability of the past seven days. It had been almost two weeks since the feed-store fire. Halloween had come and gone, and people were breathing easier.

More importantly, Dina hadn't been thrust into any dangerous situations. Gabe hoped the arsonist had packed his bag of tricks and left town.

Driving into the farmyard, he took a moment to appreciate the natural beauty of the small farm. He admitted that he already thought of Dina's place as home. The house wore a casual neatness. Things were kept in their place, but not meticulously so. Her house might not pass the white-glove test but did pass the comfort one.

The only thing that truly bothered him about Dina's house was the shrine in the living room. The south wall seemed to be a permanent monument to Jerry Paxton.

Was Dina afraid she'd forget her husband? Is that why the wall looked like part of a museum?

He unloaded the groceries onto the kitchen counter. From the quiet of the house, he figured Dina was probably holed up in her workroom, trying to get ready for the craft show she had coming up on the weekend. Wally was gone more than she was home—usually taking pictures of local school events or working on her photography book at the newspaper office.

Dina had a big house and nobody to fill it.

During the time Gabe had been at the farm, he'd tried to get used to the solitude. After growing up with three noisy siblings, he knew how to appreciate peacefulness. But true contentment demanded the sound of children's voices and family camaraderie. He wondered if that was why Dina kept herself busy—so she wouldn't notice the silent emptiness.

Of course, he realized she didn't have the sort of family background he did. She'd grown up as an only child.

But now she was an only adult.

And that could easily change if Dina ever got married again and had a family. He knew she'd make an excellent mother. She was warm, sensitive and caring. All the ingredients any man could hope for in choosing a mother for his children. All the ingredients any man would look for in chosing a lifetime partner. But according to rumors, she didn't date. Had she been so in love with her husband that she couldn't bear the idea of another man touching her, making love to her? Or was Dina trying to emulate Wally's single status?

Wally was an attractive woman for her age. He'd seen many of the older men eyeing her trim figure, trying to engage her attention.

As for Dina...even dirty old men like Ralph What's-his-name had the sense to wangle dates to the movies and to try to get a firsthand peek at her lush curves. Something Gabe himself heartily sympathized with. He'd like to peer down her shirt himself. Hell, he wanted to do more than look!

Gabe gave himself a mental shake. He was lustful enough without thinking about Dina wrapped around him. When he'd agreed to move into the farmhouse, he never realized the temptation he'd be forced to endure. Hell, he hadn't even *liked* the woman.

She'd managed to keep out of his path as much as possible during the past few weeks. Not since the first morning had she come into the kitchen for breakfast. When he'd carted a load of crocks into her workroom yesterday, he noticed a discarded doughnut box in her trash basket and an insulated coffee mug. Did she think she could hide out there until Christmas? He wondered if the hiding had worked. Had she been able to shut him out of her thoughts?

His mouth curved into a humorless smile. He should be as fortunate.

Passion was stalking him. When he listened to Dina singing in the shower, his blood pressure doubled. At night, he created erotic fantasies thinking of her sleeping just a few yards away from him. It drove him crazy. And for what purpose? All indications were that she was still in love with her late husband.

He had no desire to compete against a ghost.

So why the hell was he even thinking about it?

Two hours later, after he'd lured Dina out of her workroom and into the kitchen for his home-cooked meal, Gabe found himself burning with frustration. Despite Wally's absence—she was conveniently spending the evening in town with friends—and the intimacy of the kitchen, Dina seemed distant.

If he'd hoped to seduce Dina with his fantastic cooking, he'd obviously missed the mark. Ever since they'd sat down at the small kitchen table, Dina had played with her food and barely said a word.

"Don't you like the food?" Gabe finally asked.

Dina started, the sound of his voice pulling her from the darkness of her thoughts. She looked down at the food that was still heaped on her plate and then up at the man who'd prepared it. "Sorry, I guess I'm not very hungry."

"Bad day?"

She put down her fork and gave up the pretense of eating. "I'm not very good company tonight, I'm afraid."

"I'm not company. I live here. Remember?"

The distinct edge in his voice made her realize he hadn't appreciated her answer. Hurting him hadn't been her intention. She'd seen enough unhappiness and pain today. She didn't want to be the cause of producing any more. She picked up her fork once again.

His hand clamped firmly on her wrist, stopping her half-hearted attempt to eat. "Don't feel like you have to eat it for my sake."

The warm pressure of his hand and the gentle concern in his eyes undermined what little control she had left. She had a strong urge to empty the misery overflowing her soul. She dropped the fork and sighed, but didn't pull away from the security of his touch. "There was a terrible car accident on Highway 61 earlier today." The memories were still fresh, and it was almost unbearable to talk.

He prodded her. "Was anyone killed?"

"No," she said dully. "Several people were badly hurt, though. It was an awful, grueling mess. One of the victims was a little six-year-old girl. It took us several hours to free her from the wreckage."

"What did you do?"

She shifted her shoulders in a helpless movement. She just couldn't blot out the little girl's sobs. "She was so small. So fragile. There wasn't much I could do except hold her hand, talk to her and try to comfort her as best I could." Her voice dropped to a whisper. "She cried a lot."

"You did what needed to be done. You helped her."

She wrenched her arm from the comfort of his, while shaking her head almost violently in denial. "I couldn't help her. She wanted her mother."

"Where was her mother?"

"I don't know."

"But you were there instead."

Why couldn't he see? *She* wasn't enough. "I wasn't her mother!" she retorted, unable to hold back her fury and frustration any longer.

For a moment, there was silence as she tried to get herself under control. What was the matter with her? She was a levelheaded, stable person. She never acted this way. But ever since the wall had fallen, she'd felt on edge. The accident today only added to the increasing tension.

Gabe's soft, dark-rimmed voice cut through the volatile silence. "Who are you feeling sorry for—the little girl or yourself?"

Dina's head snapped up. She glared at him. "You weren't there. I was!"

Gabe lifted an eyebrow. "Exactly. You were there. Her mother wasn't. By being there, you probably saved her from a lifetime of bad dreams. You did your job. Soon that little girl will heal and go home to her family. She'll have you to thank. What more do you want?"

She wanted to hurl his food into his face. He looked too calm, too untouched. He'd had a mother and a father. What did he know? "You don't know what it's like to be hurt and alone."

"Without a mother?" He paused. "Like you?"

She hated him as she'd never hated anyone. He had no right. "We're not talking about me."

"No, of course not." His gaze was hooded, looking as if he was trying to peer into her soul. "How did you comfort the little girl?"

She looked down at her hands, which were twisting her napkin into knots. "I told her that her mother would be there soon, and that everything would be all right. It was all meaningless babble." She caught her lip between her teeth and inhaled a shaky breath, recalling the pain of uncertainty as she'd tried to comfort the small child. Never had she felt more inadequate. Never had she felt like more of a fraud. "But I didn't know that. Not really. I just didn't want her to cry or hurt anymore even though her mother might not come. Not then. Not ever."

"Like yours didn't?"

The anger gave way to pain. She thought she'd never cry about being without a mother again. After all, she'd gotten through her wacky hormone years as a teenager without feeling sorry for herself. She'd buried her husband and later her grandfather without her mother's shoulder to lean on. For years, she'd accepted her lot and refused to bemoan the emptiness. It had taken the cries and whimpers from a little girl to rip apart the protective curtain she'd shrouded around her lonely heart and to expose her secrets and painful memories. "I fell out of my tree house when I was about nine years old and broke my leg."

His lips narrowed into a straight line. "You were alone?"

"My grandfather was working. He didn't come home until almost midnight. He was furious." A half smile curved the corner of her mouth as she recalled her grandfather's tantrum. "I realize now he was probably scared and blamed himself. But at the time, it seemed like it was directed at me."

She braced herself, expecting him to offer insipid platitudes that couldn't change the past. He surprised her. "That little girl today had it better than you did. She had you."

She searched his face and saw the deep understanding. And the deep regret, as well. He couldn't make up for the loss of her mother, but he gave her something else instead. He gave her peace of mind by making her confront what was really bothering her. If he hadn't been here, she'd probably have brooded for days about the accident. Now there was a certain sense of release. "That little girl *will* be okay," she said.

He nodded. "There's no doubt about it."

She toyed with the napkin that was now wadded next to her plate. She felt his eyes follow every movement. Her gaze met his, and she gave him a rueful smile. "Do you always get this mean when people don't eat your food?"

That laser-bright gleam entered his eyes again. "Was I mean? Would you rather that I pulled you into my arms and comforted you?"

A flush of warmth worked through her as his thumb stroked the sensitive skin of her arm. She was suddenly unseasonably warm. In the space of a few seconds, the atmosphere had changed. Gone were the regret and self-recriminations. A new awareness pervaded the room. Unbidden desires rushed forward and settled. For the life of her, she didn't know how to budge them.

Abruptly moving her chair back from the table, she walked to the trash can and scraped off the remainder of the food. The movement helped clear her head. "I'll clean up since you cooked."

"We'll both clean up." Gabe picked up his plate and joined her at the sink.

Her control wavered. He was crowding her space. She had this insane urge to paint double no-passing lines across the middle of the floor. She wasn't used to having a man in her kitchen, she tried to convince herself. She was used to moving around the big empty house by herself. That had to be the reason for her disorientation. *Yeah, but would your hormones be hopscotching like crazy if old Ralph was standing next to you?* the voice inside her head mocked. Of course not. But then Ralph Simpson hadn't saved her from being leveled by a falling wall or being roasted by a raging fire. That was something Dina wasn't used to. She knew the people of Sherman cared about her. Aunt Wally and JD loved her and were always keeping a parental eye on her, but they were her family. Gabe wasn't. Gabe was . . .

She had to pause a minute, clear her head and think. Friends cared about each other. Maybe she could safely classify Gabe as a friend. She eyed the width of his shoulders and felt the accompanying weakness in her knees, then ruthlessly ditched that theory. Care sounded insipid. It didn't account for her stampeding pulse or the way her eyes kept straying to the open front of his shirt collar.

She gulped. Gabe might have saved her from the fire, but who was going to save her from the fire *he* had started within her? She didn't have the training or the skills to put out this kind of flame.

"I'll take that platter and put it away," she said, hastily drying her hands on a towel. She walked out of the kitchen and put the latter into the china cabinet. She straightened and stepped back . . .

Into male heat.

"Oh!" she gasped, as his arms closed around her. "I didn't know you were behind me." She quickly moved away from him and in the process bumped the pictures on the wall behind her.

Gabe's hand shot out, catching one of Jerry's pictures before it toppled to the floor. But he couldn't stop the other one—the biggest picture of Jerry—from dropping.

The glass shattered and sprayed across the room. Dina dropped instantly to her knees, plucking the picture and glass fragments from the carpet.

"Watch out or you'll cut yourself." Gabe bent down next to her.

His hand brushed hers. Electricity arced from his hand to hers. She jerked back, and a piece of glass pricked her finger. "Ouch!"

Before she could put the cut to her mouth, Gabe grabbed her hand. "Let me see."

"No. It's okay. I'll be fine." She tried to tug her hand back from the warm confines of his.

Gabe refused to release her hand. Instead, he tugged her to her feet and then maneuvered her into the small bathroom. With his body pressed close to hers, he thrust her hand under cold running water and said, "Where are your bandages?"

With her freed hand, she pointed to the cabinet above the sink. "You don't need to do this. I can take over from here."

His gaze bored into hers. "Would you have left that little girl unattended if she'd been kicking and screaming?"

"Of course not," she said, understanding that he was trying to draw a parallel. "The circumstances are different. This is just a small cut."

"And I have a small need to take care of it. You know what it's like to have that need, don't you, Dina? You want to make all the hurts better, no matter how much that person resists. It's a power that can't be denied." He watched her through those intense eyes, never cutting her any slack. The need in him pulled at her. "If you kick and scream, it'll just take me that much longer to take care of it. But the ending is already inevitable.''

What was inevitable? She quit struggling, wondering how big a battle she'd lost.

A small need? If only she could believe that. His touch was warm and nonthreatening, whereas his gaze was possessive and personal. She knew she didn't have the power to stop him from treating the wound. But it was totally different from her experience with the accident victim today. With Gabe, everything was different.

In the cramped space, the muscles of his legs brushed and then trapped hers. She couldn't escape him. The male scent of him wafted through the tiny room and filled her head. Every nerve ending responded to the gentle firmness of his touch.

She held herself rigid as he leaned over, shut off the water and then checked to see if her finger had stopped bleeding. His face creased into a frown. ''We'll have to keep an eye out for infection.''

She nodded. Eager to put some distance between them, she made one final tug at her hand.

His fingers tightened. ''Hold still. Grab the other end of this bandage so I can rip it open.''

She reluctantly held her end while Gabe pulled. His hand increased its hold around hers. She inhaled sharply, her heart pounding harder than when she was trying to escape the villainous flames.

He caressed the final strip into place. ''Is that too tight?''

''It's fine. Thanks.'' She retrieved her hand as quickly as she could and all but raced from the bathroom.

Gabe cleaned up the bathroom before following her.

By the time he arrived back in the hall, the broken glass had vanished, and Dina was busy straightening the rest of the pictures still on the wall.

He pointed to the broken picture. ''When was this one taken? Your husband looks like he just won the lottery.''

For a sliver of a second, pain crossed Dina's face. Then it was gone. ''I took that picture on the day he proposed to me.''

"You must have made him a very happy man."

She turned her back on him and fussed with the frames that didn't need fussing with. "It was an important day for both of us."

An interesting evasion. Did she think that she hadn't made her husband happy? Even from across the room, a newcomer to the house would have spotted the male satisfaction in Jerry Paxton's expression.

"Why aren't you in any of these pictures?" he asked.

A guarded expression appeared on her face. "I put Jerry's pictures on the wall after he died. Because of his stroke, Gramps couldn't turn the pages of the photo albums, so I framed these pictures. He loved Jerry like a son." Gabe looked as if he was going to question her further, but Dina was through revisiting the past and old memories. "It's rather warm in here. I think I'll go out on the porch for a few minutes."

Before he could stop her, she slipped on a jacket and opened the door.

The quiet of the farmyard instantly calmed her as the full moon glowed, casting the buildings and vehicles in a fanciful light. She'd needed to escape the intimacy of the house. The more she was around Gabe, the more she found herself wishing to let down her precious guard. There was something about Gabe Randolph that made her want to unburden her secrets, and she couldn't risk that. She didn't want Gabe probing into the parts of her life she allowed no one else to see. She couldn't tell him the reason she wasn't in any of the pictures on the wall was because she couldn't stand seeing the innocent-looking girl in them. That girl had been a fraud.

She eased into the wooden porch swing.

The screen door creaked open and snapped shut.

Gabe's voice broke the stillness. "I'm sorry if I was out of line."

She should have known that he wouldn't take the easy way out. His honesty and directness were a lethal combination. "Apology accepted."

He cut smoothly through the darkness and dropped down into the seat beside her. "What did you do before you became a pottery painter?"

She couldn't carry on a normal conversation with Gabe sitting only a heartbeat away. Even the great outdoors was no match for the heat that radiated from him. She stood up and walked to the other side of the porch before she answered him. "I was the receptionist, bookkeeper, secretary and doughnut girl for the construction company that had been in my family for generations. I managed a couple years of college along the way, but I never finished. Gramps thought I was wasting time taking art classes when I could be doing real work. Jerry became Gramps's partner after we got married."

"You were the Girl Friday," he mused aloud. "I'm surprised you didn't insist on being part of the work crew."

Her lips curved into a half smile. "If you could have seen the tree house I tried to build, you'd understand why I was better off doing the book work. I couldn't hammer a nail for love or money."

She heard the swing creak as he stood up and crossed the porch. He stopped next to her. "Why didn't you find a different job?"

"Gramps and Jerry needed me," she answered simply.

"Then when they died, you suddenly found yourself with no family, no job, no future." He didn't wait for her response. "If it were me, I think I would have resented the hell out of them for making me so dependent."

His perception jolted her for a moment. She swallowed and wrapped her arms around the pole as she stared into the night. "I think resentment is too mild for what I felt. I was financially solvent because I sold the construction company for a tidy sum. But the money didn't mean anything. It couldn't make up for losing the life I'd known. I was angry, furious and bewildered. Everything was gone." She paused, and Gabe didn't interrupt her silence. The nighttime noises rose and fell. Her arms loosened from the pole. She turned around and faced him. "Isn't it ironic? You share life with someone you love, but you can't share death.''

There were few people who would have understood the hollowness she'd experienced. But Gabe did. She felt his understanding riding on the waves of space between them. The connection between them was strong. It drew her and frightened her. Buried feelings stirred to life. And none of them had a thing to do with her dead husband. She couldn't give in to the tug of desire she was experiencing for Gabe. Her strength was anchored in the emotional barriers she'd kept protectively around her. If the barriers collapsed, then she would be entirely defenseless. And forever lost.

She must never relax her vigilance.

"I'd better get to bed." Without waiting for a response, she escaped into the solitude of her house as if the fires from hell were licking at her heels.

Dina kept busy with her crocks during the next week, but the painting left her mind too free to think about Gabe. Even a blistering argument with Essie Mae at the playground meeting about where to put a new merry-go-round didn't dilute her awareness of Gabe for long. He managed to slip into her head when she was helping with preschool as she suddenly wondered what he was like with children. No matter what she did, she couldn't banish him from her mind. He crawled into her thoughts uninvited. Since the fire station had been quiet all week, she didn't have anything else to keep her mind occupied. Even Aunt Wally, who spent more time in town than she did at the farm these days, didn't provide any relief from Gabe's presence.

Physically, Gabe was impossible to ignore. The crocks in her workroom were stocked daily. When she had trouble getting satisfaction from her pottery supplier about a delivery, Gabe tracked down the president of the company and then handed over the phone to her so she could demand some answers. He never interfered; he just made life run more smoothly for her. She got more done in one week than she had any other week since she'd started her business. Everything ran on oiled wheels except for her heartbeat. Her heart hadn't marched to a regular beat since he first stepped foot in her yard.

There was no doubt in her mind that Gabe Randolph was more dangerous to her peace of mind than any arsonist threatening to destroy Sherman. Gabe's brand of fire was twice as lethal. She battled her growing desire for him. Maybe she should kiss him and get him out of her system. Then she wouldn't be daydreaming, yearning for the touch of his hands and wondering about the taste of his mouth.

He didn't make it easier for her to control her wild imagination, either. Gabe had been changing her Beach Boys cassette tapes whenever he delivered her crocks, replacing her music with some of his tapes. It wasn't that she minded the music of the Doobie Brothers or the Moody Blues, but Gabe's cassettes just made her more aware of him. Made her think about him. Made her dream about him.

He had developed some nasty habits that played havoc with her senses. Whenever he was within twenty feet of her, he found some excuse to make physical contact. Handing her the telephone receiver, he made sure their fingers touched. Electrical currents couldn't be as strong as the heat waves that flowed between them. If Gabe held the door open for her, she would suddenly find him standing so close that she had to brush by him to cross over the threshold. Her arms tingled for hours afterward. She couldn't get the feel of him, the memory of him and the awareness of him out of her mind. She would almost welcome a midnight fire alarm—a false alarm, of course—as an excuse to escape the smoldering awareness that swirled through her own house.

She hadn't had a decent night's sleep since Gabe moved in.

Her only relief came at the biweekly fire drill for the volunteers, which was more demanding than usual because of the recent fires. She had no choice but to block out everything except the intense practice even though she hated the reason why.

After all the equipment had been stowed away, JD called all the volunteers into his office for a short meeting.

"What's this about, JD? Any word about the cause of those fires?" Tim Gimble asked.

JD walked around to the front of his desk. "The investigators believe it's someone local. They want all of us to keep our eyes and ears open. If you hear anything unusual or suspicious, report it to me."

"Do they want us to go door-to-door and check people out?" one of the other volunteers asked.

JD shook his head. "That's exactly what you aren't to do. If this person feels like he's being pressured, he might set off another fire. We haven't lost anybody yet, but there are no guarantees about next time. For the safety of every man and woman in this room, don't do any investigating on your own." He stopped as his gaze swept the room. His eyes met Dina's and held them for a moment. She could see the worry and concern clouding his expression. His gaze moved on. Finally he said, "That's all for now. I hope I don't have to see any of you before our next practice."

A rumbling of comments accompanied the volunteers as they crowded through the door. Dina hung back, hoping to speak to JD. But he was in a deep discussion with another fire fighter. Then with another. She couldn't quite escape the feeling that JD was deliberately trying to avoid her. After a few more minutes, she gave up waiting and followed the remainder of the group out the door. She would talk to JD tomorrow and find out what in the heck was going on.

Dina didn't notice the brisk evening temperature as she trudged down the road, with the full moon to guide her. She was so intent on the thoughts churning through her head that she didn't notice Gabe walking toward her from the opposite direction until she almost ran into him.

"Is this a private walk or can anyone else share it?" Gabe's voice came to her in the darkness.

She looked up and recognized the familiar form of his large shadow. She shrugged and then realized he couldn't see the motion. "The road is public domain."

They walked for a few minutes, not speaking, their feet scuffing the loose pebbles. As they turned up the lane, Gabe broke the silence. "Still trying to solve the problems of the world?"

Her laugh was short and humorless. "I don't have time to worry about the world. Sherman has more than enough problems of its own these days."

Even through the darkness, he could feel her tension. He'd come looking for her as the night hours deepened. If she was too long out of his sight, he tracked her down. He needed to know she was safe. But he didn't tell her his qualms. "Has JD figured out who knocked over that wall?"

"It might have been an accident" was her too-quick response.

"Sherman seems to have had more than its quota of accidents lately," he said with measured evenness. Getting her back up would only produce more defense barriers and make her push away. He couldn't afford to have her fight him. He'd entertained the idea of seducing her, hoping the heat of passion would be enough to keep her at home and out of harm's way. But although the seduction would alleviate some of his own raging desire, he didn't have a clue how Dina would react. If she didn't punch him in the gut, would passion be enough to make her stay clear of the town for a while and tend her own needs? His stomach tightened. She would probably still want to go out and nurture the whole damn town. Dina Paxton wasn't just any woman. She was a woman with a mission. A mission that outdistanced any desires a normal woman would have.

Her eloquent sigh interrupted his mental skirmish. "We've always been such a quiet community. I don't know why anyone would want to destroy that."

Or hurt Dina. He wisely kept that thought to himself. "Greed can be a strong motive."

"Greed?" The saliva in her mouth tasted bitter. "Would money make you risk depriving your friends and neighbors of their homes or livelihoods?"

He had no words of comfort to offer her. The odds were that the arsonist was a member of the community. He knew only one person in town who might have something to gain from the fires. "Did the mayor want to sell his buildings to you?"

Dina drew her coat more tightly around her and quickened her pace. "Sure. Why not? He almost sold his Main Street property about a year ago to an outside developer who was interested in opening a gambling casino, but the town council wouldn't agree to it."

Gabe frowned. "That must have been a lucrative deal. How did the mayor react when it fell through?"

She hesitated. "He didn't seem upset, but Essie Mae was furious with the town council."

Gabe digested this information before he asked, "What are you going to do with your craft-store plans now?"

She shrugged her shoulders and frowned in thought. "I don't know. It all just seems like such a waste. Those buildings were useless for so long. Your restaurant has brought in some out-of-towners. It seemed like a good opportunity to bring in some more new business. But now the buildings are gone, and to rebuild them would cost a fortune. There aren't that many options available anymore."

Gabe silently agreed.

They finished the rest of their walk in silence. Arriving back at the house, Dina walked up the steps of the porch and collapsed on the swing. Gabe anchored his leg on the railing and looked down at her.

Her beauty was as natural as the moonlight. Her face was expressive and freely revealed all the emotions that pulled at her. The urge to protect her was strong, but would she let him? She used all her passion for the well-being of others. It was a damn shame. "Have all the women in your family been so community-minded?" he asked.

An unladylike snort escaped her. "Wally has always told me that there are those women who are born to marry and have children. And then there are those women who are born to raise a ruckus. I guess the Cassidy women have always preferred to make their mark on the world. No wonder I have such a small family tree."

Gabe thought he noticed a shade of wistfulness in her expression. "Is that why you decided to adopt the whole town?"

"You sound as if you don't approve," she said. It didn't matter what he thought. Her life had always been very fulfilling. She knew her future would be, too. If she doubted it, all she had to do was look at the fullness of her aunt's life. Wally hadn't needed a man to make her life complete. Dina's own life would be similar.

"The only person who needs to be happy with your decision is you." Suddenly he reached over and touched her cheek. The warmth of his hand startled her.

"Why did you do that?" Her voice came out a whisper.

"Just making sure you're real."

"Why wouldn't I be?"

"I don't think I've ever met anyone who's collected so many halos in such a short lifetime." The deepness of his voice sent shivers through her.

"Halos? I'm not that noble."

"No?" His tone was quizzical but his gaze was dark.

Dina shook her head. She was no saint. Her motives were as selfish as the next person's. "Someone has to take a stand against the twisted person trying to control us."

"It's always frightening to lose control, isn't it, Dina?"

She caught his double meaning, and moved away from him. "For some more than others."

His voice followed her. "What are you so afraid of, Dina? You have your life all safely planned. Your passion is saved for the underprivileged and the downtrodden. All your barriers are in place. Nothing can hurt you."

But you can, she cried silently to herself.

Gabe was making her feel the sharp-edged thrill of a woman's desires. She wanted to run and hide. A web of desire that had nothing to do with the moonlight was drawing her to him, undermining everything she believed in. Passion bestowed its own brand of poison. Hadn't the price for marrying Henry VIII been the death of Anne Boleyn? Hadn't passion ultimately caused the despair and deaths of Romeo and Juliet? Gabe was wrong for her, and she for him. The binding tentacles of desire could strangle them both if they weren't careful. Why was he doing this? "Don't try to pour me into the void your brother left in your life, Gabe," she pleaded.

"What's between you and me has nothing to do with my brother." The deep power in his voice reached out to her. "I won't hurt you, Dina."

Yes, you will, the voice of conviction shouted within her.

Chapter Five

Three days later, after Dina dropped Wally off at her Women's Club meeting, she drove to Sherman City Hall. She had decided to present a new proposal to the mayor. Several area residents had approached her and were anxious to have a retail outlet for their locally made products. They were counting on her to open a store in time for the Christmas shopping season.

She opened the door to the city hall and was nearly toppled over by Billy Bob, Essie Mae's nephew, as he came through the door.

"I'm sorry, Dina. I didn't mean to knock you over." The ever-charming Billy Bob reached out and steadied her. He gave her a grin that would probably seduce ninety percent of Sherman's female population.

Dina was in the other ten percent. Billy Bob's carefully groomed gold locks, stylish black leather jacket and country-club polish did nothing for her.

"Are you all right?" he asked.

"I'm fine," she said. "I didn't realize you were in town visiting your aunt and uncle."

"I was passing through the area and I just popped in to say hello. I'm on my way to the airport right now." He looked at his watch. "Oops! I've got to run. Why don't we catch a movie the next time I'm in town?" He gave her another one of his aren't-you-lucky smiles.

She shook her head in exasperation. Didn't he ever give up?

Before she could respond to his latest invitation, however, he was racing down the steps. He gave her a wave. "Catch you another time."

Not if I see you coming first was her unspoken thought. Fortunately, Billy Bob didn't breeze in and out of town too often. He considered Sherman too rustic for his city-slicker tastes.

Stepping inside the musty-smelling city hall, she discovered the mayor's office was empty. She walked around the corner and poked her head into the town treasurer's office. "Hello, Kordelia, is the mayor around?"

Kordelia Simpson, who was bent over the trash basket next to her desk, whirled around with a shriek. "Oh my stars, you scared me. Why would you do such a thing? Didn't that aunt of yours teach you any manners?"

"I'm sorry," Dina said as she watched the little birdlike woman twist the circulation out of her hands. Though Kordelia was Ralph Simpson's older sister, sometimes it was hard for Dina to imagine that both of them came from the same set of parents. Ralph was a charmer who never had a nickel in his pocket, whereas Kordelia rarely smiled and hoarded Monopoly game money. That's what made her the ideal town treasurer. "I didn't mean to frighten you, Kordelia. I thought I'd check and see if the mayor was free."

"He's not here," she grumbled. "He went to the Cities to see his stockbroker."

Dina raised her eyebrows in surprise. "I just met Billy Bob on the steps so I assumed that he was visiting the mayor."

Kordelia jerked her head in a negative motion. "Billy Bob stopped by on his way out of town. He didn't stay but a minute." She shuffled some papers aside, seeming rather restless and uneasy.

"Are you okay?" Dina frowned. There was something about Kordelia's agitation that wasn't normal. She usually had her spectacles glued to the ledger, made short work of small talk and ran city hall with a tight fist wrapped around the reins. Now the little woman didn't seem to be able to relax.

Kordelia's eyes shifted nervously to the trash basket next to her desk and then focused again on Dina. "I'm not sure what to do."

"About what?"

"I came into the office this morning and found these." Kordelia stepped aside and pointed to the basket.

Dina peered into the gray aluminum receptacle, expecting to see nothing more sinister than a dead mouse. She didn't anticipate finding a wad of wrinkled, soiled white sheets inside. She reached down gingerly, picked one up and held it to her nose. The smell of gasoline permeated the air.

Kordelia hovered nervously at her side. "Do you think...?" Her voice crackled. "Do you think someone wanted to start a fire here?"

"I'm sure it's nothing serious. But why don't you call the fire chief anyway, Kordelia?" Dina tried to keep her voice calm so as not to alarm the older woman. But her stomach clenched as the implications set in. Had Kordelia interrupted the arsonist? Had the city hall been the next target?

"Oh my Lord!" Kordelia wailed. "They're going to burn us all alive, aren't they?"

After Wally decided to stay in town, Dina headed home two hours later, her mood as gloomy as the gray clouds looming nastily overhead. Her shoulders and back ached as if the weight of the world rested on them. She'd had a heated argument with JD after he'd arrived at city hall. He'd refused to put her on night patrol duty. When she'd asked for more details about the ongoing investigation, he'd put her off, telling her that he would talk to her later. She hated being at odds with JD on top of everything else.

The sight of a camper with a Minnesota plate and a large variety of colorful stickers plastered on its windows parked in front of the house did nothing to lift her spirits, either. She wasn't in the mood for company.

Inside the kitchen doorway, she came to an abrupt halt. Seated around the kitchen table were Gabe and a couple who could only be his parents.

She viewed them with more interest than she had any right to.

The older man—about Gabe's height and stature—got to his feet. If she'd hoped Gabe would be wrinkled, bald and stooped in thirty years, her wish wouldn't be granted. This man had the same ageless appeal as Sean Connery. But, thankfully, he didn't make her stomach do aerobics or give her heart fits like his son. He was just a pleasant, ordinary man. He thrust a large hand toward her, and she found her small one encased in a cocoon of warmth. "You must be Dina," he said.

She nodded. "And you must be Gabe's father."

"Ouch!" he said. "You don't think I could pass for his brother?"

"Quit flirting with the poor girl, Glenn." The woman with Gabe's deep, mesmerizing eyes stood up next to her husband. As small as her husband was tall, Mrs. Randolph bypassed the handshake and gave Dina a warm hug instead.

"Dina, I'd like you to meet my parents, Glenn and Naomi Randolph," Gabe said. "They're on their way home from a jaunt to the East Coast and decided to stop and check on their lost son."

Gabe pulled a chair out for Dina as Naomi and Glenn returned to their seats.

"I hope you'll forgive our intrusion." Naomi wore an earnest, hopeful expression. "But we wanted to see how Gabriel was doing."

"You're welcome to visit anytime, Mrs. Randolph." Dina gave Naomi a warm smile. Naomi Randolph was a hard person to resist. She obviously had a lot in common with her son. "I'm sorry about your son, Danny. This must be a difficult year for you."

Naomi's eyes moistened with tears but she managed a wide smile. "Please call me Naomi, Dina. I'm sorry to be a wet noodle. I guess a mother never gets used to losing a child. We all miss Danny so much, but at least we were able to have twenty wonderful years. Some families don't get that much."

"That's true." Dina's voice dipped to softness. "Life isn't always fair, is it?" She had little experience with nurturing matriarchs whose families dominated their lives. Yet she felt a surprising bond with Gabe's mother. Dina understood Naomi's grief and admired her strength to recover following her son's death. From the corner of her eye, she saw Gabe move his arm protectively around the back of his mother's chair. It was an unconscious action that said so much about Gabe and his family.

Gabe's father cleared the hoarseness from his throat. "We didn't come to Dina's to cry all over the floor, Naomi."

Naomi reached into her purse and rummaged through a wide assortment of paraphernalia. She emptied a few items on the table. "You're right. Excuse me while I find a tissue. I cry over everything these days. I went into the service station to pay for my gas, and when I saw the service manager wearing a baseball cap like Danny's, I started bawling. Poor dear, he didn't know what to do, so he handed me the oil rag from his pocket."

Everyone chuckled while Naomi set a packet of pictures on the table. Dina recognized Gabe in the top picture. "May I?" she asked.

Naomi nodded. "That's a picture of Gabriel and Danny. It was one of the few times I got a picture when Danny was standing still. No doubt Gabriel had hold of the back of Danny's shirt."

Dina studied the two brothers. Both were the same height. But Danny appeared lankier and wore a more earnest expression on his face as he gazed off to the side as if his attention was on something other than the camera. Gabe, on the other hand, stared directly into the camera. Even in a picture, you sensed his stability, determination and sense of purpose. Dina glanced up to meet Gabe's intent gaze. "He looks like you."

He gave her a wry grin. "Poor Danny." He reached over and picked up a picture his mother had placed on the table. "Is this the latest picture of Susan's baby?"

Naomi finally found her handkerchief and wiped her eyes clear before leaning over to take a look. "Oh, yes, hasn't she grown?" Naomi turned and beamed at Dina, sharing her pride. "Susan is our daughter, and this is her baby, Samantha. She has Susan's eyes."

"Along with Danny's adventuresome spirit and Gabe's determination," Glenn added. "A lethal combination. It was bad enough that there were two of them. But put them in one body and this country will never to be the same. You wait and see if I'm not right on target."

Dina tried to squash the slight tingle of envy at Glenn and Naomi's parental joy. Dina had had a happy childhood. Gramps had done the best he could. But there had been times when she had yearned for a traditional family. They were unrealistic fantasies, though. She'd learned the hard way that she and tradition had very little in common.

Glenn patted his son's shoulder. "We stopped in town at the fire station to see JD, but he wasn't around. The black holes left by those fires don't do much for the local landscape, do they? Does JD have any notion about who's behind these fires?"

Gabe shook his head. "There are few clues. The only thing they know for sure is that the Sherman fires bear some striking similarities to several fires that have occurred in other Midwestern cities. But none of those cities has had more than one fire. Sherman has been the only community to suffer the effects of two fires."

Dina's eyes widened with surprise. This was the first time she'd heard of comparisons between Sherman's fires and any others outside the community. She knew JD and the investigators had been secretive about the facts of the case, but obviously Gabe shared some of that privileged information. She tried not to let it bother her.

Naomi cast a worried gaze toward her son. "The restaurant isn't in danger, is it? You will be careful, won't you?"

Gabe squeezed his mother's shoulder. "Whoever is starting these fires is targeting only empty buildings. No one's been hurt."

"So far. There's no guarantee that the next fire won't claim a life or two," Naomi said with a slight catch in her voice.

"The town is trying to take extra precautions," Dina hastened to assure Naomi. Too many lives were at stake. The older woman had already lost one son. They had to catch the arsonist soon. She intended to corner Gabe after his parents left and find out what he knew and why JD had told him instead of her.

Glenn stood up. "Naomi, my love, it's time we bid these folks farewell."

Naomi rose to her feet, giving Gabe a reluctant smile. "Yes, I suppose it is."

Gabe dropped his arm around his mother's shoulders. "You'll have to give the kids hugs for me."

"They miss you. We all do. Will you be able to come home for Thanksgiving?" Naomi gazed up into her son's face with undisguised longing.

A heavy dose of regret covered Gabe's expression. "I know how much you'd like to have us all together this year, but the restaurant is having a big Thanksgiving dinner the night before. I doubt if I'll be able to get away."

The loss of hope on Naomi's face was more than Dina could bear. "Why doesn't your family come here for the holiday?"

Surprise and delight creased Naomi's face. "Are you sure you want the whole Randolph tribe descending on you?"

Dina thought it would be safer to have the whole Randolph clan under her roof than to deal with just Gabe. She caught Gabe's narrow-eyed expression and knew he suspected she was eager to have his family as a buffer between them. She stifled her guilt and gave Naomi a bright smile. "Does your family like pizza takeout?"

Glenn slapped Gabe on the back. "Gabe can cook. He's better in the kitchen than Naomi is."

Naomi continued to look worried. She must have noticed her son's reticence. "You're such a sweet girl, Dina, and your invitation is very kind, but don't feel that you have to put yourself out for the sake of the Randolphs."

Dina touched the other woman's hand reassuringly. "We'll expect you all on Thanksgiving morning."

Naomi turned to her son. "This will be just perfect, won't it, Gabriel?"

"I'm sure it will." Gabe responded with an edge of grimness as his cynical gaze met Dina's.

What are you afraid of? his gaze asked.

Dina wasn't brave enough to confront the answer and broke the eye contact.

Five minutes after his parents left, Gabe took a call from Wally and then tracked down Dina in her workshop. He leaned against the door frame. "JD's bringing Wally home later so you won't have to go in and pick her up."

Dina didn't look up. "Okay."

"You charmed my parents."

"They're nice folks." She looked up and smiled. "I'm sure Aunt Wally and JD will enjoy their company for Thanksgiving. It's been only the three of us for every holiday since Gramps and Jerry died. It will be a nice change of pace."

He nodded, and then a frown deepened the lines on his face. "You looked rather tense when you came home. What happened in town?"

Dina sighed as she recalled the chaotic scene she'd left behind. "Kordelia Simpson discovered rags soaked with gasoline sitting inside her wastebasket at city hall."

"How long had they been there?"

"She claims the basket was emptied last night."

"What about the mayor? What did he have to say?"

"He wasn't there." Dina rubbed the back of her neck.

Gabe crossed the floor. His fingers brushed aside her hands as he kneaded the taut, painful muscles around her neck. For a moment, she resisted the relief and the sensational warmth he provided.

"Relax," he growled. "So Kordelia interrupted the arsonist?"

"It looks that way. The other fires weren't started with gasoline, were they?" She shook her head, trying to keep the facts clear in her mind while his hands were touching her. "You didn't tell me the fires were similar to others outside Sherman. Do they think the same person set those other fires?"

"No one knows anything for sure. There's no hard evidence."

"Why didn't JD tell me?"

"Perhaps he thought you had enough on your mind." He jammed his hands into his pockets and considered her through brooding eyes.

She laid down her paintbrush. "I feel like I missed something—something right under my nose. Maybe I should go into town and take a look around city hall again."

"Did you happen to talk to JD before you left?"

The quiet darkness in his voice made Dina's neck muscles tighten again. "We talked for a few minutes but then we were interrupted." She didn't like the grimness in Gabe's expression. Suddenly she recalled JD's evasiveness after the feed-store fire. He'd been withholding something from her and she suspected Gabe knew what it was. "What's going on? What didn't JD tell me?"

There was a pause, then he said, "The editor of the newspaper received an anonymous letter several weeks ago. He received another one yesterday."

"What kind of anonymous letter?"

"Along with a lot of wild threats, the writer implied that a certain fire fighter was certain to meet *her* death if she didn't stop interfering."

"She?" She inhaled sharply as a chill raced down her spine. She tried to analyze his words, but they had no meaning. "The writer meant me?"

"There's no other woman volunteer in the department."

She carefully set aside the crock she'd been painting. If she hadn't, she would have dropped it with her shaking hands. "Why didn't JD tell me this before?" Her confused gaze swung up to meet his.

"He thought it might be a prank at first. But then the editor received a second letter this morning."

"JD thinks the notes are legitimate?" she asked slowly.

"After you were nearly killed by the wall, JD has to take this threat seriously."

"What's he going to do?" The words tumbled from her mouth in a monotone fashion as if she still couldn't comprehend the significance.

"Until they capture the man with the torch, JD wants you to take a leave of absence from the department and sit tight."

"He can't be serious!" She jumped to her feet. A pounding tormented her head. "That's no solution. How can JD even suggest we give in to this madman who's manipulating the town?"

Gabe's expression, if possible, became darker. He tracked her agitated pacing but made no move to stop her. "Right now, we don't have any choice. The safety of the entire town might be at stake. Nobody wants to give this guy an excuse to start another fire. Do you?"

An angry buzzing filled Dina's head. *No!* This couldn't be happening. "Everyone's in danger because of me, and I'm not supposed to lift a finger to stop it! I can't just sit back and twiddle my thumbs." She shook her dazed head. "Why do you know so much? Why is JD talking to you instead of me?"

His lips tightened with impatience. "He received the second call from the editor yesterday when I was in the office."

Dina rubbed her arms, trying to ward off the chill that had nothing to do with the room temperature. "I could still help with the patrols."

"No, you can't."

Her gaze narrowed as she eyed him with sudden suspicion. "You're behind this, aren't you? You went to JD and demanded he do this, didn't you?"

He didn't deny it. His closed expression never changed. He looked as impenetrable and as unmovable as a giant boulder.

"Damn you!" she whispered.

He didn't flinch. But a bleakness covered his face. Then he was gone. The door shut behind him, signaling Dina's isolation from the rest of the world. She found herself alone with her rattling crocks and a wave of cool fall air. She didn't remember when she'd been so mad or so miserable. The worst of it was that she couldn't forget the expression on Gabe's face. How could she have been so cruel? She knew he was merely trying to keep her safe as he hadn't been able to do for his brother. She'd thrown his protectiveness back in his face because she couldn't handle the responsibility of his caring so much.

Lord knows, she didn't deserve the shelter those big arms offered.

She was a prisoner, she concluded three days later. Not a physical prisoner because she could still go anywhere she wanted, but she was an emotional prisoner. And Gabe seemed to be her jailer.

The stacks of crocks in her workroom continued to be refilled, but it was as if a ghost did all the work because she never saw Gabe. For a big man he'd become extremely adept at disappearing into thin air. And that only made her more aware of him than if he was right underfoot.

She tried not to think about the arsonist or the fires. But the more she tried not to think about them, the more she did. She'd finally contacted JD, but he refused to reinstate her, assuring her that the other thirty-five volunteer members in the department could handle any emergencies.

Of course they could. But she didn't like knowing she was so expendable. To make matters worse, JD had also discouraged her from making any unnecessary trips into own—which she interpreted to mean she was supposed to stay away from Sherman.

She felt as if she'd been cut off from life, and she'd never been so miserable. It wasn't enough that her aunt, who could come and go as she pleased, kept Dina updated about the town's goings-on. Just knowing she couldn't respond to a call was driving her crazy. Even with a paintbrush in her hand, she felt useless. She was furious that she was being controlled by some faceless person. Being a rescuer had given her life a purpose. She was of value to the community. *And she needed to feel needed.* Helping others was the life she had created for herself.

A certain numbness after Jerry's death had protected her from feeling too much at one time. Now she didn't feel numbness. Only deflation, emptiness and loneliness.

She hated this period of suspension. JD would never have agreed to this if it hadn't been for Gabe.

Allowing Gabe to stay at her farm had been a flat-out mistake. Nothing had been the same since he'd arrived three and a half weeks ago. Evidence of his presence was everywhere. Two pairs of Gabe's shoes sat next to the front door. The bathroom was always damp and male-scented in the morning. When he was in the house, his whistling through his teeth rang through all the rooms. He'd upset her job, her environment and even her digestive system. She'd never eaten so many meals that contained all the basic food groups. Her list of things-to-be-fixed had ceased to exist. Even the forklift was once again operational.

Gabe Randolph was taking over. He was infringing in areas she considered sacred.

She knew Gabe had taken several calls from JD about the fire. JD hadn't asked to speak to her, although Gabe did pass along his greetings. It reminded her of the time when Jerry had gone to work for her grandfather. Her place in her grandfather's life suddenly changed. She was pushed to the background while Gramps began to rely heavily on Jerry, grooming him to take over the business.

She'd hated being jealous then.

She wasn't handling it any better now.

The second night of her banishment, while her aunt wa
out of town at a photographer's convention, she received
panicked call from Alice Withers. The older woman though
she'd seen someone loitering suspiciously in the street an
she wanted Dina to come and take a look.

When Dina tried to leave, Gabe blocked the door.

"Where are you going?" he asked.

"Alice Withers thought she saw someone strange in he
neighborhood." She pulled on her jacket.

Gabe didn't move. "Why didn't she call the sheriff?"

"She's afraid to make a fool of herself again after sh
called the fire department and claimed her house was o
fire."

"Why call you?"

She gritted her teeth. "She knows that I'll come."

Gabe sighed heavily. Finally he gave an abrupt nod. "Al
right. Call her back and tell her that I'm on my way."

She frowned. "What?"

"You don't want to put Alice in any danger by riskin
having the arsonist see you, do you?"

"You're not a fire fighter." Her bitterness rose like a ser
pent.

"This isn't a fire." He walked toward the door. "Stay ou
of trouble."

"Trouble?"

Gabe stopped dead in his tracks. He slowly turne
around. "You still don't get it, do you?"

His narrow-eyed gaze drilled through her defenses
"What are you talking about?"

"JD isn't cutting you out of the action. He's protectin
you." He said the words slowly as if he were talking to
dim-witted child.

Her back stiffened. "I'm not going to discuss JD wit
you."

"What's the matter? Scared you might learn some
thing?" Gabe moved closer to her. His deep, hypnotizin
eyes seemed to see right through her.

"I think you'd better leave," she said, in hopes of divert
ing him.

He shook his head. "Take a good look at your father-in-law the next time you see him. The fear is aging him minute by minute."

Her chin lifted. "He's trying to save this town."

Gabe shook his head. "No, he's trying to save you. He's scared to death that the next fire will be your last. He's scared he's running out of time and he won't be able to protect you."

Tears filled Dina's eyes. Words rose to her lips, but her throat closed, and she was afraid if she opened her mouth she'd break down and cry.

"He needs you, Dina," Gabe continued forcefully. "And he's terrified he's going to lose you again."

"Again?" Now he wasn't making sense.

Gabe tipped her chin up with his index finger. "Maybe JD believes he not only lost a son three years ago, but also the woman whom he loved as a daughter. Think about it."

He didn't wait for her response but opened the door and disappeared into the night.

She stomped around the house for the first half hour after he left, berating the absent Gabe and mentally calling him every name she could think of. Finally she ran out of steam and out of names, then she collapsed on the couch and started thinking about the meaning behind Gabe's words.

She knew her father-in-law hadn't begrudged her her success as an entrepreneur or fire fighter—he'd actively supported both. But over the past year, JD had been prodding her to date again. He'd even suggested she redecorate the wall displaying the photographic images of Jerry.

A picture of JD's face rose in the back of her mind as she recalled his pained expression. "Where's your sense of adventure, Dina? Where's your spontaneity? You've become so controlled, I barely recognize you anymore."

She hadn't understood what he was trying to tell her then.

Had a fundamental part of her died at the moment when the fire killed Jerry?

Dina picked up a pillow and hugged it against her chest. A wave of sadness swept through her. Yes, she was differ-

ent. She could admit she'd lost a vital part of herself. B
unfortunately, she didn't think she could ever go back to th
old Dina. That innocent, naive girl was gone forever. An
for good reason.

The telephone suddenly rang. When she answered it, sh
recognized Gabe's voice on the other end. "Alice Wither
is okay. She only spotted a teenager loitering under th
neighbor's tree waiting for his girlfriend to meet him."

"Alice is okay?"

"She's starting to calm down. I'm going to stay around
while," he said.

His generosity touched her. "Thank you," she said softl
into the receiver.

His voice was gruff. "Are you okay?"

She knew what he was asking. "I'm all right."

He hesitated for a moment. Then he said, "I'll see you i
the morning."

Dina slowly replaced the receiver into its cradle. Why wa
she suddenly wishing Gabe was coming home to her no
instead of staying with Alice Withers?

By Friday, she was ready to climb the walls, even thoug
the past two days had been more productive than she'd ex
pected.

She'd finally talked to the mayor about her craft sho
again. He'd grudgingly agreed to sell her the old bakery a
a reasonable price after complaining. "That group of in
vestors offered me a hundred and fifty thousand last yea
for that empty store."

"The property's not worth that much money," she re
minded him. He'd made the same complaint when she'
offered to buy the machine shop and later the old farm-and
feed store. "Even though you won't make as much from th
sale of the bakery, the craft store will bring in visitors to th
community."

The mayor had grumbled in response, but finally agree
to sell her the last empty building on Main Street.

She'd barely managed to rest the receiver in its cradl
when the phone rang again and she recognized Essie Mae'

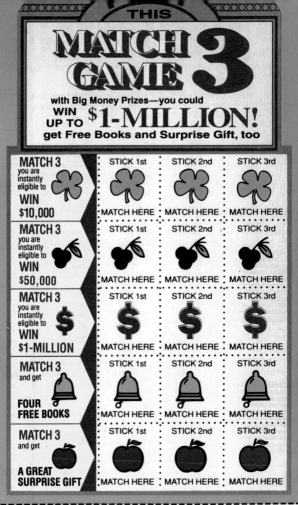

LUCKY STARS

Everybody's got a Lucky Star & this may be yours. SCRATCH GOLD FROM BOX & STAR. You're definitely in – you qualify for a chance to win the Super Bonus Prize revealed.

HAWAII
2 WEEKS

▲ PRE-FOLD BONUS GAMES & SEPARATE AT DOTTED LINES — PL

Extra
EXTRA

Super
DOUBLE BONUS PRIZE

Prizes on these Games are BONUS EXTRAS, all for 1 winner, AND on top of outraged voice on the other end. "The new choir robes arrived for the high school students and they're awful, just awful."

Dina rubbed the bridge of her nose. "What's wrong with them?"

"It's the color" came the huffy, outraged reply. "How could you order that putrid, grisly purple? I told you to go with the sunflower gold. It's much brighter and classier."

"We decided to let the students choose the color of the robes, and they wanted the purple because it's their school color, remember?" Dina tried to keep her voice agreeable yet firm.

Essie Mae hung up in her ear.

Dina sighed after replacing the telephone receiver once again. Continuing to serve on committees with Essie Mae resembled a nagging toothache steadily increasing in pain. She certainly didn't need the aggravation of locking horns with Essie Mae every other day. And the mayor's wife didn't show any signs of letting up on her animosity toward Dina. It wasn't worth the tension.

She should perhaps consider quitting some of her committees. Before Jerry's death, she'd only been on a handful. Since then, that handful had grown to fifteen or so. They'd become an unhealthy crutch. Maybe JD was right. She needed to cut back.

On the other hand, tangling with Essie Mae briefly took her mind off her growing awareness of Gabe for a few minutes. But it wasn't long enough.

Why couldn't she ignore him? Was she experiencing the hostage-captor syndrome in which she was finding herself drawn to the man who was responsible for her being grounded? She'd never been around a protective man before and it was a stuffy, confining and exhilarating experience. He made her feel both safe and unprotected at the same time.

In spite of herself, she was attracted.

For both their sakes, she couldn't act upon that attraction. It reeked of potential disaster. A woman didn't flirt with a dangerous man like Gabe. He came with binding ties.

Soon he would be looking to settle down. He would want a marriage like his parents'. The stay-at-home wife, kids and hot meals three times a day.

Dina wasn't the traditional little housewife. She thought kitchens should be declared a no-woman's land, and recipe books were written in code. Her female role model had been her footloose, independent Aunt Wally. At one time, Dina's greatest wish and biggest obsession had been to have a houseful of children. She'd wanted to hear children's laughter ringing through the big house with a driven desperation. But that obsession had led to her greatest heartache and her never-ending guilt.

Since then, she'd learned to accept her lot in life and her empty nest. She could only be what she was.

She stood up and paced to the window. Outside was the same view she'd seen all of her life. Beautiful, peaceful and oddly stagnant. Today she couldn't find anything soothing about the familiar terrain. It seemed only to reinforce what she did not have.

Pacing wasn't alleviating the stress and tension building inside her. She had to get away from Gabe.

For the time being, all of her activities in Sherman were either canceled or off-limits. Aunt Wally had offered to give up her card game and stay home to watch a movie with her this evening, but Dina had refused to have her aunt give up her own plans.

Of course, there was no reason why she couldn't cross the river to La Crosse and do what any other single woman would do on a Friday night. Throwing down her paintbrush, she went into the house and placed a telephone call. She almost smiled as she hung up the phone.

Tonight she had a date. By tomorrow, her life would be almost normal again. She could be content.

At least she hoped that would be the case.

The movie might have been a hit comedy, but Dina thought the funniest scenes came from the audience and not in the action on the theater screen. Shortly after she and the near-deaf Ralph Simpson arrived at the theater in La

Crosse, two older ladies sat down next to them. The middle-aged woman sitting next to Ralph spent most of the movie swatting Ralph's creeping hands off her knees. When the woman tried to rebuke him in a loud whisper, Ralph tapped his hearing aid, indicating he couldn't hear what she said. Dina suspected the woman was enjoying Ralph's attentions. The movie house wasn't full; the women could easily have moved to different seats. If Dina wanted for this evening to keep her mind off Gabe Randolph, the fires and anything else, she had succeeded.

Later, Dina and Ralph stopped at the drive-in café for root-beer floats before crossing the river and heading back to Sherman. By the time she arrived home, Dina felt mellow, almost content. She'd needed a break. Being with Ralph always took her mind off everything else.

Climbing down from the van, she was surprised to see Gabe's truck parked under the big elm tree. Lights shone through the living room drapes, and it wasn't quite ten o'clock. Friday nights were the busiest of the week for the restaurant. What was Gabe doing home?

"Have a nice time?" she heard him ask before she'd pulled the door closed behind her.

Turning toward the couch, she found him stretched out across the entire length. Her gaze hungrily took in the picture he made with his denim shirt unbuttoned halfway down the front of his chest and his shirttails hanging free from the confines of his worn jeans.

"I had a very nice time. Thank you." Was it her imagination or was there a sense of danger in the air? The countrified living room that was warm, open and friendly by day shimmered with a sensual intimacy. It was hard to breathe normally. She nervously fingered the silver pin on her coat.

Gabe's eyes narrowed. "Another trinket from Ralph?"

She thrust her chin out. "Ralph likes giving gifts. Refusing them hurts his feelings."

"Earned another halo, did you?"

He didn't make it sound flattering, and she decided it was a good time to change the subject. "Is the restaurant closed tonight?"

He shook his head slowly. The dim light from the lamp perched on the end table caught the gleam of his white teeth. Wolf's teeth, she thought warily.

"My employees told me they'd quit if I didn't get out of there and leave them alone. So I gave myself a night off." Again the flash of teeth.

She decided she would do what Red Riding Hood should have done immediately on encountering the wolf. Retreat. She started toward the stairs.

"Running?" he taunted.

"In my own home?" She placed one hand on the smooth wood banister.

"Where are you going in such a hurry?"

"It's late. I'm going to bed."

He swung his feet to the floor. There was nothing sluggish in his stride as he crossed the floor to her. Just force and purpose. "Aren't you going to ask me why I'm really here?"

She licked her lips. "Why?"

"The past few days, I've been waiting for a break in the ice," he said. His gray eyes were dark and sensual. "I've been patient, biding my time. I knew that you needed time to get past your anger and time to reevaluate your life. But then instead of coming to me, you go out with your good old buddy, Ralph. Tell me, what's the attraction there?"

"There's no attraction between us." She pushed herself away from him, not liking his tone or his insinuation. "I never told you to hang around waiting for me."

"Your tongue might say a lot of garbage, but your eyes haven't been nearly so obscure. There's a growing attraction between us, and you know it. We've been tiptoeing around it and it hasn't gone away. I've been giving you time to adjust to me and to rearrange your priorities."

"There's nothing wrong with my priorities. I was doing quite well before you blew into town." Dina tried to sound firm. "I don't know what you thought you saw in my eyes, but I only have friendship to offer you. If you want more than that, there are plenty of local women who might be eager to show you the sights in town."

Gabe's gaze glinted. "None of them would rescue a poor old blind dog from a blistering fire." He leaned forward. She found the next step of the staircase and eased onto the higher elevation. "None of them has snapping green eyes that play havoc with my breathing."

"Have you tried brown eyes yet?"

He ascended to the first step, bringing his body within breathing space of hers. She found the tantalizing air hovering between them as erotic as if he were actually touching her. "Brown eyes have a certain appeal. But then I'd miss the saucy tongue and the spicy sense of humor."

Her foot searched and found the next level. "You could find someone who's more agreeable. Someone who knows how to cook."

He claimed the second plateau. "Agreeable women lack a certain spark I've become addicted to, and I don't need a cook."

"What makes you think I want you?"

"Tell me you don't, and I'll leave." His grim command demanded her honesty.

She couldn't form the words with her lips. His mouth hovered enticingly near hers. She moistened her lips and trembled.

"What is it you want, Dina?" he coaxed.

Everything! her soul demanded. Her heartbeat rose to her throat. She wanted him, but she was scared. What would he expect from her? What would she have to give up? "I don't want anything," she finally managed to say.

Gabe moved closer to her. He brought his hand to the side of her face and cupped her jaw. His gaze was intense with demand and need. Her own desires mirrored his.

She had been cold and alone for so long. She'd convinced herself she could live without affection. But suddenly she thought she'd curl up and die if this man didn't take her in his arms and kiss her.

Her tongue darted out and wet her lips in anticipation as his face came closer. A flame of need torched her belly.

"Do you want me to kiss you, Dina?" he asked hoarsely.

"Do I have to tell you?" His words worked like an aphrodisiac on her senses. The movement of his hands drove her crazy. She didn't want to think. Feeling seemed so much more powerful at the moment.

His face came closer. She lifted her mouth, preparing for the first taste of Gabe. Then through her half-closed eyes, she saw him stop.

"Yes, I think you do." His tone bordered on a husky growl. "Before God, your husband, your grandfather and whoever else is watching from Heaven, do you want me to kiss you?"

Coldness zapped through the fog of desire. The mention of Jerry and Gramps brought her down to earth as nothing else could have. Pushing against his chest, she stepped back. She took deep, jagged breaths, struggling to find her way back through the sensual haze and lingering intimacy.

"You're right. This is a mistake." She wished her voice was steadier.

His hand fell to his side, but he didn't move away or release her from his penetrating gaze. "I didn't say it was a mistake. But I don't want the past standing between us."

She clenched her fists at her side. "The past can't be erased. It teaches us harsh lessons and makes us who we are."

"What lessons did you learn, Dina?" The words were soft, but tinged with a distinct edge of impatience.

She didn't want to face the question, let alone answer it. But she knew she didn't have the inner emotional resources to deal with a reprisal of this scene. She needed Gabe's cooperation if they were going to escape this kind of fiasco again. "I'm not capable of making the kind of commitment that a man needs."

He shifted, blocking the light. "What kind of commitment is that?"

She gritted her teeth and strengthened her resolve. "You'd ultimately demand more than I can give."

"Is that what happened with Jerry?"

Pain and anger surged through her. She grabbed for the anger. "Jerry loved me and I loved him. We'd still be married if he were alive today."

Gabe never flinched. "Who are you trying to convince? Me or yourself? Do you think he'd expect you never to love again?"

"Jerry has nothing to do with this."

"You're right, he doesn't." Gabe closed the space between them again. "This is between you and me. No one else is involved. I don't want to be lumped with all the other needy souls you're already taking care of."

Her mouth tightened. "Where did you get the idea I take care of needy souls?"

The corner of his mouth lifted with cynicism. "You've given yourself over to the needs and concerns of everyone else and kept very little for yourself."

Why was he crowding her? "I don't need much." She couldn't contain the edge of desperation that colored her words.

"Don't you? Everybody admires and respects you, but they don't know you're using them, do they?"

She jerked as if she'd been slapped. Hurt lodged itself deep inside. How could he even suggest such a thing? "I've never used my friends and family." She tried to slip around him and escape down the steps.

Gabe grabbed her hand and held her still. "Those needy souls are your first line of defense. You hide behind their problems and don't have to face your own."

She held herself rigidly. "What makes you say that?"

"You think I don't know the courage it took to find meaning in just getting out of bed in the morning after your husband died? I can almost admire the life you've created for yourself. But what part did you keep for yourself?"

She searched his face and saw the pain and the strength of a man who had survived his brother's death. Gabe Randolph met life head-on. He was a very strong man. A woman could get sucked in by his sense of invincibility, making her weak and dependent. That kind of vulnerability terrified Dina.

"I don't owe you any explanations," she said.

He dropped her hand. "When are you going to quit hiding from life, Dina?"

For a moment, she hesitated, then she tilted up her chin. "You call it hiding. I call it living."

Gabe went still. Dina wondered at the battle waging within him. She held her breath, hoping he'd make the right choice, but unsure what the right choice actually was. Would his own control snap? Would he haul her into his arms and kiss her, fanning the blaze starting inside her? Or would he walk away and leave them both aching and unfulfilled?

A hard expression crossed his face. Gabe stepped back down the stairs. "Go to bed, Dina. I can't compete against a ghost and the whole damn town for your attention."

Dina heard the disgust in his voice, but kept mute. He was wrong. He didn't have to compete with the whole town. He was first and foremost in her thoughts, and it scared the living daylights out of her.

His frustration was hers. Yet she felt as if she owed him something. "I'm sorry, Gabe. I never meant for any of this to happen."

For a moment, he remained stiff and unyielding. His eyes were wary and searching as if he doubted her sincerity. Finally he stepped down another step. "That makes two of us, doesn't it?"

Suddenly the front door opened. Wally walked in with a troubled expression darkening her face. The drawn lines didn't lighten when she spotted them on the stairs. "Dina, there you are. JD tried to call you earlier."

Dina pushed past Gabe. "What's wrong?"

Wally laid a hand on her shoulder. "While you were in La Crosse, the old bakery started on fire."

Dina's feet were already in motion by the time Wally finished the sentence. Jumping into the van, she barely noticed Gabe slip into the passenger seat next to her.

She drove straight to the bakery.

Gabe yanked open his door before the vehicle came to a stop. But Dina couldn't move. The sight that greeted her sapped her dwindling energy.

Where the old, brick-faced bakery had stood, only the partial side of one wall remained. The grocery store next door had lost two windows but was still standing. Fiery ashes covered the surrounding area. A hose shot a stream of water at the embers as JD and several volunteers prowled through the rubble.

With weighted limbs, Dina left the van and moved toward JD. He saw her and grabbed her arm to move her away from the others. "Dina, the fire's under control, but I'm going to have to talk to you."

Frustration and fear burned within her. "It's all my fault, isn't it?"

Her father-in-law shook his head. "You know better than that. The only person at fault is the person torching these buildings. But you might be the key. Or at least someone is setting you up to make it look that way."

Chapter Six

While Gabe drove, Dina refused to think. She didn't move, didn't say a word during the entire trip back to the farm. Her mind was as empty as the burned shell of the building they'd left behind. She didn't want to face the black reality of what had just happened and how she might be responsible for the latest terror.

Gabe stopped the vehicle in front of the house and plucked Dina from the seat, swinging her into his arms. She didn't have the energy to protest as he placed her on the couch and flung her coat onto the chair. He hauled her next to him and began rubbing the circulation back into her hands and arms. "Come on, Dina, talk to me."

She resisted, but he wouldn't let her pull away.

Gabe tried to think of ways to cut through Dina's resistance. He knew she was taking the blame for the fires, but he couldn't understand why. He could deal with defiance, anger and even wariness, but he couldn't handle the defeat he was seeing on her face. The lack of energy—so unlike Dina—scared him. He didn't know how to make her open up to him, either. But he had to try. "That fire wasn't your fault. You weren't even in town when it broke out."

She didn't seem to hear him, and then, after a long moment, she said in a lifeless voice, "I put a down payment on the bakery yesterday."

Gabe's head reeled. "Why the hell didn't you tell me?"

She lifted her shoulders. "There was nothing to tell. Nothing had been finalized."

"How many people knew?"

"It wasn't supposed to be a secret." Suddenly her stomach cramped, and she bent over in pain. "What if somebody had died? It would have been my fault and I don't even know why."

"Nobody died," he forcefully reminded her. "The only person responsible is the arsonist."

She shook her head. Seeing her loss of hope and animation knifed Gabe. She stared at him but he didn't think she was actually seeing him. "You don't know what it's like."

"What what's like?"

"Living with the guilt of another person's death on your conscience. Knowing that if you had been a better person or had made different choices, that person might still be alive." Suddenly she turned and looked him fully in the face. Her face was pinched with anguish. "I couldn't go through that again."

Gabe didn't believe for a moment that Dina was guilty of anything. Hell, if there was ever an angel on earth, it was Dina. He refused to believe she'd hurt anyone. "You've done more for the people in this town than they deserve."

She looked down at her white-knuckled hands. "A couple of months before Jerry's death, we had been having marital problems. Jerry wanted me to devote more time to helping him expand the business. But I was ready to quit being his Girl Friday. I wanted to have a family. I wanted to be a mother."

"Jerry didn't want to have kids?"

She shook her head. "He was an only child and felt uncomfortable around children. I thought he'd eventually change his mind. But he didn't and I refused to back down. We argued almost continually." She splayed her fingers as if at a loss for explanations. "The tension was killing both of us."

"What happened?" he prodded.

She leaned her head back on the couch and closed her eyes for a moment as the old pain flooded through her. "The day of the fire, we'd had another terrible argument. We were at the construction site. It was a new house, and Jerry was working in the bedroom closet on the second floor. Usually my grandfather was there, but he wasn't feeling well and had stayed home that day. Jerry and I started arguing about having children again. He told me to get out and leave him alone if our marriage wasn't enough to keep me happy. So I left."

She caught her lip between her teeth in an effort to regain control over herself. "I drove straight home, but I didn't want to tell Gramps about the argument so I hiked up the bluff and tried to work through my anger. When it started getting dark, I walked home and found JD and Gramps waiting for me with the news that Jerry was dead." She swallowed and looked down at her white-knuckled fists. "Jerry's death almost killed my grandfather. He blamed himself for not being there. But in truth, I was the one who abandoned Jerry. My obsession for a child made me leave my husband. He died, and a few months later so did my grandfather. Through my negligence, I killed them." How could she have been so stupid and selfish?

Gabe's hands tightened around her shoulders. "It was an accident. You couldn't have done anything. Do you think Jerry would have blamed you?"

She shook her head. "It doesn't matter whether he would have or not. If I hadn't been so pigheaded, he wouldn't have been there alone. He was right. I should have been happy with just our marriage. I wanted too much, and I lost everyone I loved most." The losses had been ruthless, devastating and final. How could she have ever believed she'd have made a good mother if she was such a negligent wife and granddaughter?

She hadn't understood until then how painful love could be. She didn't ever want to hurt that badly again.

In the past, having a child had been her greatest desire. Now the thought of having a baby terrified her. She was scared to death of losing a child as she'd lost everyone else. What if she turned her back and the baby drowned in the bathtub? Nobody or nothing could pick up the pieces of her broken soul if something like that happened.

Dina's vulnerability tore at Gabe. He wanted to throttle Jerry Paxton. Why wouldn't a man want to enjoy all the fruits of a marriage with a loving woman like Dina? If he'd been offered the gifts Paxton had been given, he'd have taken them with both hands and praised the Lord for the blessing.

Gabe had to clear the tightness from his throat before he could speak. "Maybe your husband should have been more understanding of your desire to have a family."

She knew he was right, and on a certain level she'd accepted that both she and Jerry were responsible for their unhappiness. But there was always the question as to whether Jerry would still be alive if she'd done things differently. "If only I hadn't been so stubborn, he might still be alive. I should have been more understanding. I loved him."

"You're not to blame for the terrible fire that killed your husband any more than you are responsible for the actions of this crazy arsonist and the fire tonight." His grip on her hand was firm and steady. "I'm surprised you chose to become a fire fighter."

She looked at his hands covering hers. She made no move to pull them away because the warmth of his hands comforted her in a way she never thought possible. "When JD first suggested it, I resisted the idea. But I was without a job, and he persisted until I agreed to at least take the training. Once I started the classes, I realized I could help others. It became a mission and a need. Becoming a fire fighter healed an open wound inside me."

Having made her confession, Dina felt her spirits lift a notch.

Gabe cupped her chin, his gaze boring into hers. "Isn't it time for you to forgive yourself, Dina, and stop taking responsibility for everyone else's mistakes?"

She wished it could really be that easy. If only she could let down her guard. But the smell of smoke and ashes still clung to her skin. "There's someone out there who wants to make me responsible. How do I stop that?"

Gabe pressed her closer to him. "We'll find him, Dina. He's bound to make a mistake sooner or later, and then you can get on with your life and put the past behind you once and for all."

He only hoped they could stop him before it was too late.

Gabe's watchfulness increased during the next few days. Something had changed between them, and Dina wasn't sure how to handle it.

Gabe had become her anchor. He enticed her from her workroom with a little game of one-on-one basketball. He asked her opinion about some blueprints he'd drawn up for a possible addition to the restaurant. She found herself responding to him, relying on his understanding and his stimulation to keep from sliding into a sea of despair. No suspects had been identified after the bakery fire.

The mayor had been questioned, of course, since he knew about Dina's plans to buy the bakery. But the mayor had been playing bridge that night and had an ironclad alibi. It was difficult to pinpoint if anyone else knew about the plans. A footprint had been discovered near the scene, but the fire chief hadn't been able to determine whether it was actually from the arsonist.

Dina tried to talk JD into reinstating her as a fire fighter, but he flat out refused. He was just as stubborn as Gabe on the subject. He wouldn't even let her attend the next fire practice. She was furious with both of them.

"Dina." Gabe's voice stopped her as she headed out the door three days after the fire. "I have only one load of crocks left to bring up from the shed, then you're out of bowls."

Not being able to paint would be the last straw. She needed to paint or the inactivity would kill her. She pivoted. "I'd better call the factory again. Maybe they've made a change in their delivery schedule."

A short time later, she hung up the phone, her shoulders drooping with discouragement.

"No luck?" Gabe watched her from the doorway.

"If I want them badly enough, I can drive to Chicago tomorrow and meet the driver. I don't—"

He interrupted her. "I'll drive down and pick them up for you."

For a moment, she was tempted but then she decided it wouldn't be fair. "You've done too much already. I'll have to cancel a few orders, but I can probably fill the majority of them if the next truck coming this direction delivers on schedule." She didn't have a lot of hope. Too many variables were involved to ensure the safe arrival of the pottery. Everything from potholes to a changeover in drivers could hold up the delivery. She couldn't blame the pottery company for her short stock, however. It was her own fault; she should have ordered more the last time.

Gabe crossed the room and stood close to her. The overwhelming heat of him disturbed her thinking processes. "I can leave early tomorrow morning and I'll be back by early evening," he said.

She shook her head. "This isn't your responsibility. You shouldn't have to give up your free time because of a miscalculation on my part."

"I never said it wasn't going to cost you anything."

She knew better than to trust that devilish, toe-curling grin of his. "How much?"

"A date. Dinner and maybe a movie."

"That's it?"

"Yes."

He made it sound simple—as simple as going to the movies with Ralph Simpson. But it wasn't. She was beginning to feel too much for Gabe. He was starting to become too important to her. He made her forget to keep her distance.

Even though she'd finally accepted that she wasn't responsible for Jerry's death, she still knew that she wasn't cut out for a permanent relationship with any man. She'd known Jerry all her life. They should have been aware of what to expect from one another—from marriage. But something had changed between them. Their needs and desires had evolved. She realized now there was no guarantee two people would grow in the same direction. That's where she and Jerry had failed.

She couldn't risk that kind of failure again.

She'd been devastated when Jerry had died. Recovering from that loss had taken every ounce of strength she could muster. Now here was Gabe. He filled corners of her life she'd never realized were empty. Could she recover from his exit from her life, too? Already she couldn't imagine what her life would be like when Gabe left. How would she handle her humdrum dreams and the endless days?

He'd be moving back into town soon. And she couldn't ask him to stay. The longer he stayed, the greater the risk of her falling in love with him. She couldn't fall in love. Especially not with Gabe. Somewhere deep inside, she knew loving Gabe would be twice as emotionally demanding as loving Jerry.

He would want too much.

She would want too much. She would expect even more, and then what would happen? She'd barely survived the guilt Jerry had left behind. It was better to keep herself protected and not to cross the line into caring too much. If only her body wouldn't ache from unfulfilled desires and her heart from emotional emptiness.

She finally looked up at Gabe. A special evening with him might be the only memory she took with her into the future. She wanted that memory.

Just this once.

"All right, we can go to dinner and a movie if you'd like," she said, blocking the repercussions from her mind. For one evening, she wanted to forget the past and the future. She wanted to have a good time and slip free from the controlling restraints she'd worn for three years. What could it hurt?

The mascara brush felt strange in her hand the next evening as Dina smudged and blotted a few strokes before she was finally satisfied with her effort. Peering into the mirror, she decided the tailored ivory blouse with the black split skirt presented the tamed, refined image she hoped to achieve. Cool, calm and in control. Now if she could just clamp down on the excitement skipping through her veins. She felt like a schoolgirl going to her first prom. And that was plainly ridiculous. Her girlhood days were long past. She should be feeling matronly and in charge.

So why didn't she?

Probably because there was nothing staid and settling about Gabe or her reaction to him.

She descended the staircase and spotted Gabe coming from the kitchen. She almost missed the last step. Her heartbeat took a leap and she forgot how to swallow. Once again he wore an open-throated shirt, but this time he'd traded flannel for crisp white cotton, which enhanced a well-tailored black sports jacket. A pair of nicely creased gray dress pants completed his evening attire. She didn't know whether to groan or smack her lips.

"I'm not sure going to the restaurant is a good idea." There was a notable thickness in his voice.

Her gaze collided with his. "Why not?"

"Because I'm going to have my hands full trying to keep every other male in the place away from you."

It was a relief to see she wasn't the only one a tad overwhelmed. "I've always wanted to see your muscles in action," she teased him.

"You never mentioned it before."

The kitchen door swung open and Wally stepped into the room. Dina welcomed the interruption.

"You both look spiffy. Who died?" Wally asked.

"We have a date," Gabe told her.

Dina suddenly felt chicken. "Do you want to join us?" What was she doing all dressed up and going out on a date with Gabe? Did she think that she could play with fire for one night and come away unscarred?

"Shame on you, Dina," her aunt tut-tutted. "Do I look like a wet blanket?"

"No," Gabe reassured her. His eyes challenged Dina.

Her gaze slid away from his. For the first time she noticed Wally's outfit. "Are you going out, too?" The red scarf and bright violet suit would have looked ridiculous on anyone else, but on Wally it made sense.

"I'm going to play bingo."

That caught Dina's attention. "Since when? You always said they'd have to tie you down with a steel chain before you'd play bingo."

"I'm compromising." Wally picked up an overnight bag. "After we play a couple games of bingo, I plan to introduce them to a new version of strip poker. It's called Strip To Your Wrinkles."

Wally left the house before they did.

"Thank you for that much at least." Gabe held her coat as she slipped her arms into the sleeves.

"What are you thanking me for?"

"For not volunteering that we should attend *their* bingo party."

She gave him a reproving look. "I wouldn't do that. We weren't invited. Besides, I'm selective about whom I show my wrinkles to."

His chuckle sent goose bumps up and down her spine. He took her arm, but didn't proceed immediately through the door. "I have one request."

"What's that?"

"Tonight it's just you and me. You're not to worry about needy souls or arsonists. Agreed?"

She drew in a sharp breath as an internal flame ignited and began to shimmer within her. "Conversation might be light," she hedged.

"We'll see." He gave her a grin that did nothing to calm her jittery heartbeat and steered her through the door.

They crossed the river to La Crosse.

When they arrived at the restaurant, she tried not to notice how handsome Gabe looked. Instead, she checked out the classy interior of the unfamiliar restaurant, which, to her mind, didn't have the same warmth and charm of Dare'n Gabe's. After they were seated, she asked, "Are we checking out the competition?"

He shook his head. "Tonight is my free night. We're here to relax and have a good time. It's just you and me, with no interruptions from Ralph, Wally or any of your other good buddies."

She didn't know what to say because she wasn't sure what kind of interruptions he was worried about. She picked up the menu and asked him, "Why did you name your restaurant Dare'n Gabe's?"

"Dare was a nickname for my brother Danny. It was short for daredevil."

"Was he a daredevil?"

"A former girlfriend nicknamed him Dare because he was headstrong and very passionate about life. The name stuck."

"I bet he was a fun date."

"A lot of women seemed to think so."

"And what about you?"

His eyes gleamed. "Are you asking if I'm a fun date? Why don't you tell me?"

She had no business pursuing this line of flirtation. And flirting it definitely was. She'd be wise to stick to safer subjects, but for the life of her she couldn't think of one. Common sense took a hike while she heeded the call of desire. "What do you classify as fun?"

He settled back in his chair and contemplated her. "I don't particularly care for high-risk excitement. Quiet conversation holds a greater appeal than raucous laughter and noisy bars. A good movie and going out for an ice-cream soda afterward is about all the entertainment I can handle." The lazy sensuality in his gaze snagged hers.

She gave him a considering look. "You're a hard man to resist."

He leaned forward and took her hand, wrapping it into the heat of his palm. The easy expression evaporated and in its place was uncensored need. "That's what I'm counting on."

His desire blindsided her. What exactly was he counting on? She forgot to breathe as wild emotions rushed through her. How did she escape the sensual maze she found herself trapped in? Gabe wasn't hiding the fact that he found her attractive. She couldn't look away. For tonight—for him— she wanted to be desirable.

Finally the waitress arrived at the table and gave each of them a menu. After they placed their orders, Dina searched for a safe topic. "How many nieces and nephews do you have?"

"My younger brother, Kyle, has two girls, and my sister, Susan, has a little boy as well as three-month-old Samantha."

She started to relax. "The girls are dominating the new branches of your family tree."

"So far."

"Excuse me." The waitress placed salads in front of them. Dina pulled her hand back into her lap.

She loved the way the muted light darkened his skin tones and the way his left eyebrow quirked when he was making a point. She couldn't help but be aware of the smooth movement of Gabe's tanned throat as he swallowed his food. And what nice hands he had, and how sharply exciting it was to have him sitting near her.

She'd noticed that he always wore his shirt collars open as though his muscular neck couldn't bear to be confined by a mere button—that's what the rational part of her concluded. The lusting hussy in her chose to believe that the open neckline was beckoning her to come hither, to run her fingers along the crisp white collar and to explore the secrets hidden inside the opening. Had she ever met a man so earthy, so natural, so brazenly male?

She took a drink of cooling water. "Do you miss living near your family?"

"I miss seeing the kids grow up. But distance doesn't change our ties to one another. We're still close and we always will be." He said this with unwavering confidence.

Dina looked down at her plate; a flash of longing swept through her. Gabe's words brought home something she thought she'd buried deep: a family relying on each other. It was easy to put herself in a position of not needing anyone. She'd sought the independence. But the flip side of the coin was that no one needed her, either. Oh sure, the town looked to her for solutions to some of its problems, but no one needed *her*. Plain old Dina.

"Is something wrong?" Gabe's question forced her to regain her bearings.

"No." She resurrected a smile.

"May I take your salad plates?" the waitress asked.

Dina nodded, thankful for the diversion. By the time the main course arrived, she felt more like herself again. She enjoyed the food and the stimulating conversation they shared. Finally she shoved aside her plate.

"You'll get to meet them," Gabe said.

"Meet them?" she echoed.

"The whole clan's coming for Thanksgiving, remember?"

She nodded. "That'll be interesting. It was nice of your mother to bend tradition so they could all come and be together."

He chuckled. "My mother's relieved that she doesn't have to cook. She's not one to cater to tradition if she doesn't have to."

Dina flashed him an answering smile. "No wonder I liked your mother so well."

"The feeling's mutual."

Suddenly Dina didn't feel as comfortable with the conversation. She grabbed her clutch purse and slid from the booth. "Your mother doesn't really know me."

Gabe stood up next to her and tossed a tip down on the table. "Scared she might get too close, Dina?"

She didn't bother to analyze his cryptic words. It shouldn't matter to her what his mother thought of her.

Once Gabe moved out, she'd never see Naomi Randolph again. Why did that thought depress her?

The movie they saw was a romantic comedy. But half-way through the movie Dina lost track of the plot altogether. Popcorn was at the center of her distraction. She'd never realized eating popcorn could be such a sensual experience. Every time she reached into the round tub, his hand grazed hers. Maybe it was the romantic context of the movie that got to her. She didn't want to admit that Gabe's leg touching hers, his arm hugging the back of her chair, or his buttery fingers stroking hers had anything to do with her state of confusion.

On the drive home, the atmosphere inside the pickup thickened with awareness. In the reflection of the dash-board lights she could make out the details of Gabe's hands. They were strong, attractive hands. Capable hands. His fingers were long, tipped with neatly clipped nails. She memorized their look as her body yearned for their touch. She wanted them to hold her, pleasure her and put out the burning sensation deep inside her.

She wanted a whole night with Gabe. A night of memories to treasure. Just one night, so that she could put out this burning desire raging inside her.

They climbed the porch steps together but before she reached the door, Gabe spun her around and folded her into his arms. "Now you can thank me for picking up the pottery."

"I thought going to dinner and a movie was supposed to be the thank-you." Her breath formed a cloud in the cold night air as Gabe's body effectively blocked the chill.

"We ate dinner so you'd have enough energy to give me a proper and thorough thank-you." His teeth flashed in the darkness. The aura of danger hovered close. All she had to do was reach out and touch him.

She moistened her lips. He was driving her crazy with all this double-talk. "I think I could say it better inside the house."

"Probably. But it's better if you say it out here." He reached down and touched her face. His callused thumb ran across her cheek.

"Why?" She barely breathed.

"Because I plan to kiss you."

Crazy swirls spun through her head again. "Why can't we do that inside?"

His thumb stroked the side of her jaw. "If we kiss inside the house, we could get carried away, and I want more than a night in bed, Dina."

She gazed up at him. The moonlight highlighted his features: solid, steady, dependable. She'd believed in those qualities once before. When they'd been ripped from her, she no longer believed. A chill slithered up her backbone and she tried to step back, but her feet didn't want to move. "Maybe we should just forget it and say good-night instead," she whispered. "Let's not complicate things."

His arms tightened around her. "Things are already complicated. We both need this to keep everything straight. All I'm asking for is a simple thank-you."

He didn't have to ask twice. He was right. She did need to kiss him. Just once, she wanted to know the taste of him, and then she could get on with the rest of her life and be content.

She raised herself on tiptoe and slipped her hands around his neck. Her knees didn't feel quite steady. Pulling his head down toward her, she ran her tongue across the whiskered edges of his mouth. Their lips brushed together. At first with gentleness. Then with a desire to learn and memorize the other.

Contentment vanished. Intense need took over. If she'd thought that a quick taste would satisfy her hunger for a lifetime, then she was doomed. Once their lips met, her appetite for Gabe grew beyond any boundaries she recognized. In his arms she discovered the sanctuary she'd always searched for. She trespassed into a territory that was both terrifying and magical. They blended. Two halves fitting perfectly together. Her head spun as she clutched the hard muscle of his arms. His kiss gave and demanded. He made her both weak and strong. He made her feel beautiful and cherished. How had she withstood this man for so long? How would she survive the future without him?

She didn't want to think about tomorrow or her history of mistakes. Only this moment in time counted. Her hands, with a mind of their own, rippled through the thickness of his hair. The world tilted. The air sweetened. By the time their mouths separated, their breathing clouds were thicker and more pronounced. Her head whirled. His arms still didn't release her, and she didn't want them to. Ever. This was the interlude that her dreams had promised her. She wanted to savor this moment with them.

"Thank you," she breathed.

"For what?" His gaze darkened and held hers.

"For everything." Her hand touched his cheek. "For this. For tonight. For yesterday and tomorrow."

This time, Gabe lifted her to meet his lips. This time, he took full charge of her mouth. Giving her all of himself and withholding nothing. She was instantly seduced by his honesty and blatant need.

The late-autumn night transformed into sultry summer. With Gabe, she felt both secure and out of control at the same time. Her hands crept inside his shirt collar and stroked the curls of hair at the back of his neck.

He slowly lowered her to the porch floor. They were both breathing heavily. She stepped back, although it felt as if she were going the wrong way on a one-way street. She suddenly felt separated from herself as if she'd been split in two. Without meaning to, she shivered. She shouldn't have kissed him. He was far more devastating than she'd ever imagined.

"Was that thank-you appropriate?" she whispered through the night air.

"It was a start" was his husky reply.

She licked her lips and tried to still her rocketing pulse rate. Somewhere along the way, things had gotten out of hand. She needed to regain control so she could face him again in the morning. "I'm afraid that's all I've got to offer."

"Do you think you can stop this fire that's blazing within us?" he asked.

"We have to." She wished her voice sounded a little stronger and more confident, as if he hadn't just knocked her world off its foundation—which he had.

"Dina—"

She made a stab at cutting him off. "Why haven't you found a nice woman and married her by now?"

She knew she surprised him by the way he started to reach for her and then dropped his hand. "I never found the right woman," he said. Then he surprised her. "Why haven't *you* remarried?"

She shook her head and took a step back. "I've been married once."

"And you still love your husband, is that it?"

She could have lied and ended his sensual stalking, but she'd never been able to lie, not even to save her own skin. This man had saved her life twice. He'd protected her and cooked for her. She owed him her honesty. "I'll always carry Jerry in my heart. But no, I'm not still in love with him."

Gabe's hands started to reach toward her once more. She sidestepped them. "It's chilly out here. We'd better call it a night."

His silent frustration followed her escape into the house. For her own peace of mind, she didn't look back.

Later, as she battled insomnia, she decided that if he had designed the evening to make her more aware of him, he'd accomplished his purpose tenfold. By the end of their night out, she'd wanted him on every level possible for a woman to desire a man. He'd stimulated her with his conversation and she'd never enjoyed an evening more. And later...his kisses...

Her face heated as she recalled the combustibility of those embraces. Had she really thought she'd be content after kissing him? How naive of her. Instead of being appeased, she wanted more. So much more. And as a result she couldn't sleep. Not even keeping meticulous count of sheep leaping fences did the trick.

There was an emptiness inside her she couldn't quite explain. Her lips ached but her heart was what was causing her the most pain. She felt ... unfulfilled. Dissatisfied. Hungry.

She finally scrunched up an extra pillow and, clinging to it, tried to pretend it was Gabe providing the comfort. Sleep still eluded her, and as a result, she heard Gabe when he left his room and walked down the hall. But he didn't stop and test her door. Unfortunately.

"Did you have a good time with Gabe?" Wally asked Dina the next morning at the breakfast table.

"Yes, I did," she said. Gabe was nowhere in sight this morning, and for that Dina was profoundly grateful. She wasn't ready to see him.

Wally poured herself a cup of coffee. "Gabe makes a great cup of coffee, doesn't he?"

"Gabe Randolph is Mr. Magic, all right," Dina said, forcing a neutral tone into her voice.

Wally gave her a sharp look. "His magic seems to have fallen flat with you. You never used to be such a grouch in the mornings."

"You know I'm not a morning person."

"Morning person, my foot. You're attracted to Gabe, and it's got you in a tailspin."

Dina's back stiffened in denial. "I'm worried about getting all of my orders completed, that's all."

"So hire a few more painters," Wally demanded. Then a crafty expression crept onto her face. "Or maybe you're not finding those crocks such warm bedfellows after all."

A flush worked up Dina's face. She drummed her fingers against her bowl. Then she grabbed the saltshaker and twirled it between her palms. "We still have an arsonist running loose while I've been having to sit here twiddling my thumbs."

Wally shook her head. "You know there's plenty of people to do the patrolling in town. Now you have no excuse not to face yourself and concentrate on what you want in the future. Forget the past, honey. You were made to have a family and a home.''

Dina feigned an expression of horror, hoping to divert her aunt's attention. "Since when did you become a traditionalist?''

"Bite your tongue. I'm not a traditionalist." Wally's voice carried a mild rebuke.

"You're starting to worry me, Aunt Wally," Dina sighed. "Next you'll want me to take up knitting, when in truth, you know that my life's just the way I like it.''

"Is it? Do you ever think about marriage?'' Wally asked abruptly.

Dina almost choked. "Not on my good days.''

"Why not?'' Wally persisted.

Dina stared at her aunt. She had a feeling that Aunt Wally's thoughts weren't centered in the kitchen. "I've been married. I know what it is to have dreams for the future and then to see those dreams destroyed by failure,'' she reminded her aunt flatly.

"You never used to be such a coward, Dina.''

Wally's words stung; they harbored too much truth. Dina had never been able to lie to her aunt. Finally she admitted, "Okay, I'm scared.''

"Good." Wally dropped her bowl into the sink and started out the door.

"What do you mean 'good'?'' Dina called after her aunt.

Wally stopped and gave her a long look. "Being honest with yourself is the starting place. Just keep working on it and you might be surprised what you learn.''

"You're speaking with the voice of experience, I presume? The woman who's worn her independence like the national flag.'' She tried to temper her cynicism.

Wally's youthful expression of optimism collapsed. She suddenly looked very much her age. "We all make mistakes, honey. Some of us just take longer to realize them.''

Later that morning, Gabe showed up in Dina's workroom—looking too good for her peace of mind.

If she thought the dawning of a new day would banish the heightening tension and awareness between them, then she was sadly mistaken.

If she'd hoped the bright sun would erase this hunger and rechannel her thoughts, she didn't even come close to attaining her wish. The desire to be with him—to spend more time with him—was increasing in intensity with each passing hour.

If she'd hoped Gabe would give her a break, she was doomed to disappointment. After coaxing her out of her workroom, he persuaded her to go with him to a La Crosse grocery to help him shop for the Thanksgiving meal the next day. She'd never realized how much fun a grocery store could be. They loaded the van with an incredible amount of food and then drove home and unpacked it together.

That evening, Gabe hooked up his VCR to her television, and they watched a hit movie with Aunt Wally.

And after her aunt went to bed, he built a fire in the fireplace, then one within Dina, before he broke the kiss and sent her to bed. Alone.

Chapter Seven

No fire could be more hazardous to her state of well-being than the one she was battling on the home front, Dina admitted as she stared out the window on Thanksgiving morning. Gloomy gray clouds were hovering overhead while large wet flakes of snow drifted aimlessly to the ground. Everything appeared bleak and depressing, including her own spirits.

She was afraid she was falling in love with Gabe, and she didn't know what to do about it. She couldn't seem to escape the sensual webs spinning around her, and worse yet, she couldn't resurrect the burning drive to fight them.

Thankfully, today she'd have a house full of Randolphs. She craved a little breathing space and a new distraction. Ten extra people filling the house should do the trick.

The first group of Randolphs arrived at eleven o'clock with laughing children, stomping feet and booming voices. Then the door opened again, and another crowd of new faces surged in. Dina found a baby plunked into her arms. The curly-haired baby took one look at Dina and started screaming.

"Oops! Sorry about that." A tall, dark-haired woman scooped the baby out of Dina's arms. "Samantha just woke up from a nap. She'll warm up to you in a few minutes."

Dina sympathized with the baby. "A strange face is frightening."

The woman grinned in agreement. "I'm Susan, Gabe's sister. You must be Dina."

Dina nodded, immediately responding to her friendliness. Susan had the easy charm of her parents. "It's nice to meet you. Welcome to Sherman."

"You're brave to take us all on at one time," came the laughing reply.

Gabe stood in the middle of the group, catching the coats and hats being heaped into his arms. There was a liberal dispensing of hugs, good-humored backslaps and playful pokes. The chattering was nonstop. Dina doubted that any of them heard a single word anyone else said as the house blazed with a strong sense of family togetherness.

"Hi, I'm Christina." A little girl with a cap of blond hair and a pair of blue button eyes stood boldly in front of her. "Do you have Nintendo?"

Dina dropped down to Christina's height. "No, I don't have any video games, I'm afraid."

The little girl sighed. "That's okay. Neither do I. We'll find something else to do."

A smaller girl peeked around Christina. She, too, had big blue eyes but instead of blond hair she had bouncing brown curls. "It's starting to snow. Maybe she has a sled."

"Don't be so shy, stupid," Christina said in a grown-up voice. "This is Janey. She's my little sister."

Dina swallowed her smile and greeted the girls with a polite seriousness. "It's nice to meet both of you. I think there's an old sled in the shed. We can check later if you'd like."

"Okay," both girls agreed.

"Aunt Wally has hot chocolate ready in the kitchen. Do you like hot chocolate?"

"With marshmallows?" Janey stepped forward, her shyness forgotten.

"The big and fat kind."

"Come on, Andy. Janey, wipe your feet before we walk across the floor," Christina ordered. She grabbed the arm of a small boy hovering to one side, while Janey brought up the rear.

"You've made their day." Another woman who appeared to be about Dina's age stepped in front of her. Like everyone else, she wore jeans and a sweater. But she had a face and figure that made every other woman in the county want to scratch out her eyes. Her scooped-back hair anchored in a ponytail provided the perfect frame for her gorgeous face. "I'm Brenda. Mother to Christina—the little drill sergeant—and Janey. I'm married to Kyle, Gabe's younger brother."

Dina, for some irrational reason, was extremely glad that Brenda was safely married to Gabe's brother. "Your daughters are delightful." Dina pointed to the container Brenda carried. "Do you want me to take that for you?"

"I baked a couple of pies. Just point me to the kitchen, and I'll check on the troops. By the way, how did Gabe con you into inviting the whole clan?"

"Knowing Gabe, he probably seduced her with his cooking," Susan said.

Gabe overheard her. "Quit giving away all of my secrets."

Susan leaned forward and whispered loudly so that everyone could hear. "We won't hold it against you, Dina. We're all suckers for Gabe's cooking. He learned at a young age that women can be manipulated by a man who can cook. That's a word of warning from one woman to another."

Dina pasted her smile into place. Even though the two women invited her to share in their private joke, she felt a shade of uneasiness. She wondered if they thought she and Gabe were anticipating a permanent relationship. She was having enough trouble keeping her distance without adding that kind of misunderstanding on top of everything else.

Before Dina could set her straight, however, Brenda winked and said, "Stick with us. We'll donate our vast knowledge about the Randolph men. We're experts."

"Who's an expert?" a man's voice intruded.

"Kyle, I thought you were helping hang up the coats," Brenda said. "Meet Dina. This is my husband, Kyle."

"Great to meet you, Dina." Kyle juggled several brown paper bags. He looked a lot like Gabe but had a leaner build. He gave her a thorough, assessing once-over. "You're just as pretty as Gabe said you were. Do you want to have an affair?"

Brenda jabbed her husband in the ribs. "Stop trying to make Gabe jealous."

"Dina's too smart to fall for Kyle's sleazy style." Gabe appeared at Dina's elbow. His arm brushed hers and didn't move away. "It amazes me that he suckered you, Brenda. You used to be a smart woman."

Brenda sighed. "What can I say? He caught me at a weak moment."

"Ouch!" Kyle glared mockingly at his wife and brother. "Stabbed by a double-edged sword. Better watch out, Dina. This is a ruthless family. I've got the scars to prove it."

"Poor baby." Brenda patted her husband's arm. "Let's see if you can hobble to the kitchen and unload all those goodies you're carrying."

Kyle shot a malicious look at his brother. "I think we've got enough food to last us a month. Better beware, big brother, we're moving in."

"Don't get too comfortable," Gabe growled. "Those brown paper bags can be repacked as easily as they can be unpacked."

Dina frowned at Gabe and was about to comment on his unfriendly manner, but just then Susan interrupted them to introduce her husband, Edward.

Edward gave Dina a sympathetic grin. "Don't take any of them too seriously. They're a pretty harmless bunch."

Dina managed to drum up an answering smile while wondering how many years it had taken him to reach his conclusion.

"I think we've done enough damage here." Brenda gestured toward the kitchen. "Fall in, troops. I'm leading the way to the kitchen."

The Randolphs had only been in the house five minutes, and Dina was winded. She saw Gabe look at his watch and scowl.

"You have something ready in the oven?" she asked.

Gabe snorted. "Nope, I'm just counting the hours until they all leave again."

This time it was Dina's turn to deliver a poke. "They've just arrived."

He groaned. "Don't depress me."

"It's wonderful to see you again, dear," a familiar voice said.

A pleased smile lifted Dina's mouth. "Mrs. Randolph, I'm delighted you've come. Happy Thanksgiving."

The gray eyes similar to Gabe's twinkled. "Mrs. Randolph sounds frightfully old and formal. I still have all my teeth so I only answer to Naomi."

Dina's face relaxed into a freer smile. There was something very appealing about Gabe's mother.

"Dina, I do declare, you've grown even prettier since the last time I saw you. How is that possible?" Gabe's father's voice boomed. The salt-and-pepper-haired man reached over and gave her a big hug.

Dina laughed. "I knew you were coming this time. I put on my Sunday best."

"Glenn, tone it down. The acoustics work quite well in this house," Naomi scolded her spouse, but her rebuke lacked a convincing punch.

"She's still trying to keep me in my place after all these years. But I only talk loud to keep her attention focused on me." Glenn's whisper was just about as loud as a normal speaking voice. "I don't need an army of men sniffing around my Naomi."

"He talks loud so he can be the center of attention," Naomi grumbled.

The couple's sparring was obviously a familiar argument. But their mutual respect was blazingly clear. Love coated every word, every gaze.

Glenn turned and gave Gabe a hearty slap on the back. "It's great to see you again, son."

"How were the roads?"

His dad shook his head. "Not good. The snow's beginning to pile up on the ground and it's still coming down steady. The wind's kicking up, too."

Naomi patted Dina on the shoulder. "Maybe by late afternoon, the sky will clear up. Dina doesn't want to be saddled with this mob overnight."

"Don't worry about it," Dina said without hesitation, ignoring Gabe's forbidding countenance. "I'd rather have everyone here than have to worry about your family driving on snowy roads in the midst of a blizzard. We have plenty of room. There are two sofa beds in the living room."

"Let's just wait and see how things develop before we start moving in," Glenn suggested.

Naomi linked her arm with Dina's. "Tell me how things are going. Have there been any new developments in tracking down the arsonist yet?"

"I'm afraid not."

"Come on, Naomi," Glenn said. "We're not going to talk about depressing subjects today."

Gabe nodded. "I second that."

Naomi gave her son a troubled look. "I just wish you weren't in so much danger."

Gabe draped his arm around his mother's shoulders. "None of us is in danger today. Everyone's safe with both JD and his ace fire fighter here. Isn't that right, Dina?" He glanced over his shoulder and met Dina's eyes with a bold challenge.

Everyone but her. She swallowed the lump in her throat. It was going to take more than her fire-fighting skills and the town's water supply to put out the flame continuing to grow inside her. Even with a roomful of people, she was aware of Gabe's every movement, his every thought. It was as if she were married to him.

A tightness banded around her temple.

Shortly after one o'clock, everyone sat down to dinner, including JD, who'd arrived a short time earlier and was sitting next to Aunt Wally. The room didn't have a spare inch in sight. The dining room table stretched as far as the added wooden leaves would allow it, and a card table had been added at each end of the table to accommodate more chairs. Nobody seemed to mind the tight squeeze, though.

Glenn offered a blessing, poignantly remembering the family's love for their lost son and brother, Danny, which brought tears to everyone's eyes. Then dishes were passed and everyone dug into the hearty meal. Dina found herself rubbing elbows with Gabe, who was sitting uncomfortably close. The room's temperature kept increasing.

"Gabriel, you're a wonder in the kitchen," Wally exclaimed after a few minutes. "This is much more appetizing than the tofu casserole that I planned to prepare."

"Tofu casserole?" Naomi questioned. "I've always wondered what a casserole made with tofu tasted like. Do you have a recipe?"

"I'll give you the recipe I found in a magazine," Wally said.

Glenn groaned. "I bet it tastes like a magazine, too. Naomi, be thankful I eat that spinach concoction you fix at least once a week. My insides aren't up to digesting this newfangled stuff."

Naomi frowned. "You know what the doctor said about the kind of food you like to eat."

"Ha." Glenn dug a well into his potatoes and poured several ladles full of rich gravy into the open pit. "You don't think that doctor's eating tofu or spinach, do you? No sirree. He's chowing down on a prime piece of red meat, smacking his lips and laughing up his sleeve at all the fools he's prescribed meals of lettuce and broccoli. Then, when the good ole doc goes to the grocery store, all the choice cuts of meat are left for him. I'll bet you don't see him eating skinless, tasteless chicken breasts."

"Look what kind of example you're setting for your grandchildren," Naomi admonished him.

"I set the same example for our sons and daughter." He grinned at Dina. "I didn't do so bad with Gabe now, did I?"

Dina felt heads swing in her direction. A flush started under the rolled collar of Dina's sweater as all eyes at the table latched on to her. She could feel Gabe's scrutiny as she floundered for an answer.

Thankfully, Brenda bailed her out. "Of course Dina would agree. Gabe has a few extra talents any woman would want. He can cook," she retorted. "When I was dating Kyle, he took credit for cooking a meal when in actuality Gabe had prepared it. Just imagine the shock when I discovered Kyle's expertise in the kitchen amounted to knowing how to raid the refrigerator."

"Hey, I know how to unscrew the lid from the peanut butter jar," Kyle protested. That was greeted by a chorus of groans.

"You should have asked me." Susan laughed from over in the corner where she was feeding the baby. "I could have told you never to trust either Kyle or Danny. They both used Gabe's cooking as women bait, they called it."

Dina stared uneasily down at her plate full of potatoes, turkey and cranberry relish. If this was bait, she was being reeled in with the rest of them. Somehow, the Randolphs' presence wasn't proving to be as distracting as she'd hoped. Even in the midst of a crowd, she felt the heat of Gabe's closeness. His gaze kept her under close scrutiny. Instead of the gathering diluting the electricity between them, she felt as if a net were closing in around her.

Damn! Gabe grimaced as he stood staring out the dining room window and watched the straight line of snow blow across the farmyard. His plans for an intimate evening with Dina after his family left were about to be kiboshed by Old Man Winter. There was no way he would send his family out into this unstable weather. It was difficult to determine how much of it was fresh snow and how much had been on the ground and was now airborne. A weather bulletin issued by

the National Weather Service interrupted the football game
that Kyle, Edward and JD were watching and advised mo-
torists to keep off the road.

It wasn't that he didn't enjoy having his family around
him. His family was special. He'd missed them all over the
past few months. But hell, he'd counted on spending this
time with Dina when she wasn't as busy with the pottery. He
figured that after a couple of months when she felt more
comfortable with him, he'd take her to Quarry City to meet
his family.

Of course, he hadn't worried about how Dina would like
his family or they her.

Just as he'd conjectured, they'd taken to each other like
long-lost relations. The Randolphs were a naturally gregar-
ious clan. And Dina, being Dina, had plunged into a game
of Old Maid with the younger members. Then she'd en-
gaged in a discussion with Edward and his dad about the
fires and the elusive arsonist. Later, she'd taken Brenda,
Susan and his mother on a tour through her workshop. She
accommodated everyone—even making sure that certain
items like the fireplace matches and other unsafe objects
were removed to a safer location, out of reach of the
younger members of the family.

On one hand, Gabe couldn't be more pleased with the
way things were going. On the other hand, he couldn't be
more aggravated. Whenever he made a move in her direction, Dina was busy with another member of his family.

It was Thanksgiving Day, and he'd never been less
thankful in his life. All afternoon he'd watched the wood
he'd cut in anticipation of a quiet, intimate evening with
Dina dwindle as his brother tossed log after log into the
fireplace. The picture of seduction Gabe had carried for
days in his mind of just Dina and him in front of a roaring
fire had given way to the reality of wall-to-wall Randolphs.

A sudden gust of wind bellowed and shook the house, and
Gabe fought the urge to roar back—only louder.

He'd intercepted a couple of smug glances from his
brother and sister. Hell, they were delighting in his misery.

They knew darn good and well they were interrupting his plans with Dina.

For the first time in his life, he was jealous of his brother and sister. They had spouses they adored and children to cuddle. What would it be like to have Dina sit across from him at the table and to claim her as his wife? To know the satisfaction that at the end of the day she'd be snuggled next to him?

Even with his family surrounding him, he ached. He wanted Dina so badly he didn't know if he could move, let alone walk. He yearned for more than quick, easy satisfaction. He desired ties of permanency. Dina made him feel things he'd only fantasized about. Settling down. Having kids. Waking up every morning lying next to the same woman for the rest of his life.

He needed all of Dina. Everything she had to offer. The excitement. The energy. The peacefulness. He wanted all the compassion his family was greedily sucking in.

Dina filled his head.

He wanted her to call his name in passion.

What would she be like in his arms? When he couldn't sleep at night, he pictured her sleeping in the next room, her body curled provocatively in the tangled sheets. It was no wonder he couldn't close his eyes. He wanted to feel her warm skin against his on a cold winter's night. He wanted to be with her, love her, explore the inner woman. Thirty years would not be enough time. He wanted fifty. Hell, he wanted a hundred and fifty if he could get it. She excited him, made him hunger for a commitment he'd scoffed at in the past with other women.

"Sorry, son, it looks like we crashed your plans."

Gabe couldn't quite tame his scowl as he met his dad's twinkling gaze. "You might be sorry, but I don't think anyone else in there minds a bit. They look like they've settled in for the duration."

Glenn chuckled. "You're probably right. They like your Dina. We all do. She's got substance. You don't see too many young women today willing to live on a farm by themselves. It shows that she's content. I like that."

"I do, too. Unfortunately, she's not my Dina."

"But you'd like her to be."

Gabe didn't bother denying it. "How'd you con Mom into marrying you?"

"I threatened to keep her barefoot and pregnant until she said yes."

Naomi came into the room just in time to overhear her husband's remark. "I promised to dismantle certain parts of his body if he tried."

Glenn's laugh echoed through the house. "Yep. So we compromised. I got barefoot."

"And when *I* was ready, I got pregnant." Naomi sent a speaking glance to her husband.

His dad grinned with no remorse. "She graciously allowed me to provide some assistance in that direction."

Gabe's grin answered his dad's. The love his parents had for each other had filled his childhood with a richness he'd taken for granted. Now he recognized how powerful their love and respect for each other was. Even through their grief at losing a son, they'd bonded together and leaned on each other for support.

"Gabriel, you need to exercise some patience," Naomi said. "Your trouble is that you're used to taking charge, issuing orders and having people do exactly what you want. Dina isn't used to that. Give her time. Eventually she'll be ready to share her life."

If only he could be so confident. "She's been married once. I'm not sure she's ever gotten over her husband's death."

His mother gave him a hug. "Dina is a beautiful girl. It'll all work out, you'll see."

Gabe envied his mother's optimism. He wished he could be as sure of what the future held as she did.

The Randolphs had settled into her home as if it were their own. Their familiarity pleased her, Dina admitted to herself. She had never felt this relaxed and comfortable before. There wasn't an uptight bone in the entire family that she could detect. It seemed as if she'd known them her entire life. The tightness in her head that she'd experienced earlier had all but vanished. Only a few passing references had been made or hinted at about her relationship with Gabe, and she'd managed to be politely vague, becoming adept at changing the subject.

Now, with the storm raging outside and the warmth of companionship inside, she could almost forget about her worries. The threat of the arsonist seemed like part of another life.

If only the same could be said about her growing feelings for Gabe. In the presence of his family the reality of Gabe emerged tenfold. The strength, the depth, the caring. He was part of them. They were part of him. She couldn't escape the fullness and richness surrounding him, and she was afraid that by the time the Randolphs left, she'd be more involved with Gabe than she had been before the day began. She sighed. Perhaps she should call 911 and have the volunteers level a cold water spray at her. How did one douse a flaming heart?

About midafternoon, JD and Glenn entered the kitchen, where the women were slicing wedges of pie. Dina was pleased to see that the two old friends were enjoying the day and catching up on old times. She'd overheard them telling Naomi and Wally some hair-raising experiences of their youth, which had probably been embellished considerably. The laughter had left their faces as they came into the kitchen, however.

"A front is stalled over us," Glenn said. "They're predicting at least another twelve inches of snow."

"Oh dear," Naomi said. "That doesn't sound good."

"They don't expect it to move out of the area until tomorrow night at the earliest. All the highway crews have been pulled off the roads, and they're telling people to sit tight. It looks like the earliest we'll be able to leave here is Saturday."

Suddenly the kitchen door swung open, and Kyle tipped his head inside the doorway. "You all might want to take a peek at the news report on television. A big fire leveled a warehouse in St. Louis early this morning. The investigators say it was similar to several other Midwestern fires, including the three in Sherman.''

Dina's blood chilled.

"Damn!" JD growled as he walked into the living room with the rest of the group close at his heels.

For once, the Randolph family was totally silent as they crowded around the television set and listened to the newscast.

"The fire that destroyed a furniture warehouse broke out in downtown St. Louis early this morning," the reporter told his viewers. "Fire inspectors investigating the fire won't know the actual cause of the fire for several days yet, although there has already been some speculation that this fire is similar to others that have broken out in the Midwest during the past couple of years."

While the reporter spoke, film footage taken of the fire played in the background. Against a raven black sky, the fire roared and dominated the landscape as bystanders watched helplessly.

Dina knew the feeling all too well.

She stared hard at the scene, trying to make sense of what was happening. The camera suddenly zeroed in on a man all dressed in black, who—unlike the other observers—was walking away from the raging fire without a backward glance. The man nervously tucked his chin into his raised collar. The camera caught the glimmer of blond hair. Gold against black. Where had she seen that combination before?

A memory teased her brain. "Billy Bob was wearing a similar black leather jacket the last time I saw him."

"He does look something like Billy Bob, doesn't he?" Wally commented.

"Are you sure?" Gabe asked. He'd never met the man, but everything he'd heard he didn't like.

Suddenly the man in black turned toward the camera, and the film captured a full face shot.

Dina frowned. "It *is* Billy Bob, but what's he doing there?"

"I don't know, but I aim to find out." JD turned around and headed toward the telephone. "I'm going to make a few phone calls."

A chill that had nothing to do with the temperature of the room swept through Dina. As much as she wanted to stop the fires in Sherman, she didn't want the arsonist to be someone she knew, either.

A lifetime passed before JD returned to the room ten minutes later.

"Well?" Wally demanded.

"The sheriff is contacting the authorities in St. Louis immediately. They'll probably call that TV station to get their film footage of the fire before they bring Billy Bob in to question him."

Wally grimaced. "Essie Mae's going to have a stroke."

JD's expression remained grim. "Probably, but this could be the major break we've been looking for. I'm going to have to get back to town. I've called Fred Ferguson, and he's sending a snowmobile for me."

Alarm raced through Dina. "Where are you going in this weather? You can't do anything tonight. The weatherman said St. Louis is getting this storm, too."

"Yes, but the fire broke out early this morning. We don't know where Billy Bob is or where he might show up next. There's plenty of time for him to get out of St. Louis and travel back here."

Dina didn't like JD's range of possibilities. She followed him to the door. "Let me go with you. We can probably get the van through those drifts."

"No. You'll be safer here."

"What about you?"

JD ignored her and looked over her head at Gabe, who was standing quietly behind her. "Keep her under lock and key. I'll give you a call when I get back to town."

Wally, looking as worried as Dina, followed JD out of the room. A few minutes later, the sound of a snowmobile could be heard above the protesting wind as the door slammed behind JD. Dina shivered as Gabe's hand imprisoned her shoulder.

"There's nothing you can do," he said. "Even if they find Billy Bob and he's the one behind the arson, he might not confess to anything."

She rubbed her arms nervously. "I can't believe Billy Bob would start those fires. He grew up in this town. He's one of us. Why would he set those fires and risk hurting the people who care about him? Why would he burn buildings I wanted to buy? None of it makes any sense." She caught her lip between her teeth. Her gaze met Gabe's. "Why?"

Gabe wished he could ignore his whole darn family loitering nearby and drag Dina into his arms. He ached to hold her and drive away the demons that still tormented her.

Just then, a large blast of wind wailed around the house, drawing everyone's attention back to the deteriorating weather. Naomi came around the corner. "I'm so sorry, Dina. We never intended to impose on you, but this weather has not cooperated, and it looks like you're going to have a house full of overnight guests."

Dina took the opportunity to slip away from Gabe. She suddenly was very pleased the Randolphs weren't leaving. "Don't worry about it. I'm delighted to have you here." She needed to have this family close in order to keep back her fears.

The pressure of Gabe's enigmatic gaze followed her out of the room.

JD called and reported he had arrived back in town safely. He'd already been in contact with the mayor and Essie Mae, who claimed Billy Bob hadn't been with them for the holiday. Dina was immeasurably relieved that there was no immediate danger. The suave Billy Bob would never venture out in weather like this. Wherever he was, it was warm, dry and far away from Sherman—she hoped. Before he hung up, JD promised to keep them posted if anything changed.

Dina returned to the living room, where the sound of popping corn rat-ta-tatted as Gabe shook the old skillet over the flames in the fireplace. The room was jam-packed with Randolphs.

The intimacy of togetherness wound through the room. Kyle and Brenda were curled up next to each other on one end of the couch. Naomi and Glenn openly held hands. Edward watched Susan rock Samantha, his love and pride plainly visible for everyone to see. What would it be like to have a relationship like Naomi and Glenn's, or like Edward and Susan's?

A firm hand pressed down on her shoulder. She looked up as Gabe swung himself onto the arm of the chair and set a bowl of popcorn on her lap. He pulled her hand and lifted it to the warmth of his thigh. Waves of heat spread through her. She knew few in the room had missed the act of possession by Gabe, but she didn't pull away. For once, she made no effort to fight him. She needed the warmth and security of his touch.

"Andy, I told you to stay away from the fire," his mother scolded. "If you're not going to listen to me, you'll have to go to bed."

Andy's chin dropped.

"Come here, Andy my boy, and you can sit with me." His grandfather patted his knee.

The unhappy little boy shuffled over to his grandfather. "Grandpa, did you ever do something that made your mom and dad mad?"

"Gosh, my memory doesn't stretch that far back," Glenn drawled. "But I guess my own dad was a bit upset when I used his shaving brush to paint the fence. He sure did look funny with white paint on his face."

"What did he say?" Christina came over and sat on her grandfather's other knee. Janey and Andy crowded closer, too.

"I don't remember the actual words, but I think most of the discussion came after a session in the woodshed."

"What's a woodshed?" Andy wanted to know.

"It's like a family room," Christina said knowledgeably.

The adults' laughter ran through the room.

"The woodshed did seem like a family room in those days, I guess." Glenn grinned. "I certainly spent a lot of time there. My sister didn't like it when I cut off all of her doll's hair, either.''

Wally overheard Glenn's comment as she walked into the room. She chuckled. "The dolls were safe from Dina. She preferred the real thing. She cut Ann Bigsley's hair when Ann's mother went grocery shopping.''

"Did your dad get mad at you too, Dina?" Janey asked, her eyes wide with fascination.

"I didn't have a dad. But my grandfather was livid," she said, recalling the scene all too clearly. "Aunt Wally told him to be thankful I'd used scissors on Ann instead of scalping her with a knife.''

"Would you have really scalped her?" The awed respect in Andy's voice amused Dina and drew chuckles from around the room.

"Probably not. The knives were out of my reach," she told him.

Gabe leaned over and blocked out the rest of the room. Only she could hear his deep-toned words. "You were a dangerous little thing, weren't you?"

"I've matured."

He shook his head slowly, his gaze pulling her into the bottomless pools of gray. "No. You're twice as dangerous now.''

"Because I can reach the knives?" she whispered.

His hand tightened around hers, trapping them in a cocoon of warmth. "No. Because you can reach my soul.''

Later, the beds and rooms were divided up. Everyone finally had a place to rest his head. The adults tolerated the spirited pillow fights and nonstop chattering of the children, who were too excited to fall asleep immediately. Eventually all was quiet except for the frenzy of winter howling outside.

Dina shared her bed with Aunt Wally. She listened to the trees creaking and bending according to the dictates of the wind and reflected on a day that seemed to encompass a lifetime. This morning it had just been Wally, Gabe and herself. Tonight the house overflowed with people—people who in the space of a few hours had become her friends. The house felt snug and content. Gabe was lucky to have such a special family. She'd experienced firsthand how wonderful that kind of life could be.

With the house full and her soul satiated as it hadn't been in years, she felt her convictions wavering again. Gabe was beginning to fill in the cracks of her life. He was starting to become too important. If Billy Bob was arrested and exposed as the arsonist, Gabe could soon move back to town into his newly refurbished apartment above the restaurant. There'd be no reason for him to continue to stay at the farm. What would she do then?

She squashed her trepidations.

For now, she wanted to enjoy this sense of family. How long this contentment would last, she didn't know. She would selfishly indulge herself and pretend it was hers.

For that's all it could be—just pretend.

Chapter Eight

The snow had lightened considerably by morning, but the relentless wind and drifts made the road impassable.

JD telephoned about midmorning to update them on the investigation. "The St. Louis police have confirmed that Billy Bob was spotted in the area of at least three other fires in the Midwest. We don't have any actual evidence in the Sherman fires, but since Billy Bob is almost a local resident, we can assume he probably is behind the fires here, as well."

"Has he been arrested yet?" Dina asked, hating the waiting and being forced by the snow to sit tight.

"There's been a warrant issued for his arrest. But this blizzard has socked in the St. Louis area, too, so they've been having difficulty determining his whereabouts."

Relief and depression swept through Dina, and she wasn't sure why. She rode high with the knowledge that this trauma could be coming to an end, and she could resume her normal life again.

But she also realized there would be no reason for Gabe to stay.

The activities that had pulled her from the time of despair after Jerry died didn't have the same appeal this time around.

Later in the morning, Dina managed to snatch a little privacy to finish one of her pottery orders. After she slipped the pots into a low oven to bake the paint, she invited Christina, Andy and Janey into her workroom. They painted their masterpieces on pots she'd previously discarded because they were too warped to sell.

"I'm going to put mine in my room," Andy told her. A few smudges of paint decorated his charming face. He reminded her a lot of his uncle Gabe. She would bet Gabe broke plenty of young hearts during his growing-up years.

"Do you think my teacher would like this for Christmas?" Janey asked, frowning at the lopsided green tree she'd painted on a small pot.

"She'll love it," Dina assured her, thinking Janey's teacher was awfully lucky to have this sweet child in her classroom. A curious wistfulness stole over her.

After they completed their painting and had a light lunch, Dina went with Gabe and the children to hunt down the sled. Old but still usable, the sled worked great on the hill at the back of the house. They made a couple of runs to pack down the snow. Sheltered from the wind, the hill was a sledder's paradise. Gabe, Kyle and Edward inflated several inner tubes to use, as well. The whole family except for Wally, Susan and the baby came out to participate in the afternoon's adventure.

Stomping the snow off their boots, the rosy-faced crew raved about the hot chocolate that Wally had ready for them when they finally came in. Susan and baby Samantha sat down next to Dina at the dining room table. Dina shoved her mug aside as the ever-active Samantha reached for the hot cup.

"Thanks." Susan laughed. "She's always one move ahead of me. I can't take her to church anymore unless I want to crawl under the pews and through people's legs to catch her."

Samantha looked Dina over closely and then spotted the old chain that circled Dina's neck. She lunged over her mother's arm to capture it.

Dina's hands automatically came out to intercept the baby leaning toward her. She was rewarded by a delighted smile from Samantha as she alternately weaved, pranced and stood on Dina's thighs. A lump lodged in Dina's throat as she braced Samantha under the arms. Everything about the baby fascinated her. The bright eyes. The busy hands. The sweet scent of baby lotion. The softness. How had God ever packed so much into one little body?

"Be careful so she doesn't break your necklace," Susan warned. "She's strong."

"It's just a piece of jewelry," Dina answered absently. Inanimate objects failed to be important next to the intriguing creature she held. She had kissable cheeks. Petal soft, Dina discovered, running her finger along the satiny smooth skin. "Her eyes don't miss a thing, do they?"

"She's a real snoop. If there's a no-no in sight, she'll find it." The exasperation in Susan's voice was tempered by a strong dose of love. She tugged the chain from Samantha's mouth. "Come on, honey. Not in your mouth. It's yucky."

Samantha giggled, mimicking her mother's screwed-up face. Dina was entranced by the special exchange between mother and daughter.

"Being a parent is the bravest occupation in the world," Dina said wistfully, continuing to balance the ever-bobbing and dancing baby.

"Or the stupidest. We adults think we're so worldly, so wise. But having a child is the fastest way to knock you off your I'm-a-mature-and-wise-adult pedestal. No one can prepare you for being a mother. I remember the night we brought Andy home from the hospital after he was born. The first time he cried, I ran down the hall to get to him. I didn't want him to cry, didn't want him to be frightened, didn't want him to face being alone."

"That sounds like a reasonable wish for a mother to experience." This time, Dina pulled the chain carefully from Samantha's mouth. Before the baby could protest, she sat

Samantha down on her knees and played patty cake wit
her.

Susan sighed. "Parents have a lot of reasonable wishes
Unfortunately, the world is an unreasonable place to brin
up children. If I'm overly protective, I deprive Samantha of
the skills she'll need in order to cope. The hardest thing
parent ever learns is that she must step back and allow he
child to take risks."

Dina looked up from her game. She'd been so naive t
believe that at one time she had the knowledge and exper
tise to be a parent. What had she really known when she'
been so obsessed with having a baby? "I'm not sure I'd b
strong enough to let go. How do you find the courage?"

Susan's gaze softened. "Support. I have a smart mon
and Brenda is a wealth of information and comfort, too. I'
be a basket case without them, and I return the favor whe
they need it. Believe me, nobody's an expert, and we're a
cowards about letting our kids out of our sight. You'll lear
the same thing when you have children."

"I'm not that brave." She wished she had Susan's cour
age to face those unknowns. When it came down to it, she'
always be wondering and worrying if she was too protectiv
or not protective enough. The very notion of somethin
happening to her child sent terror running through he
She'd lost her parents, Jerry and then Gramps. Those ha
been brutal realities. But to risk bringing a child into th
world and then having to worry about losing him or he
made her heart slam sickenly in her chest.

Just then, Samantha dropped her head back agains
Dina's breast. The baby popped a finger into her mouth
Gazing down at the snuggling child, Dina felt her throa
tighten as strong emotions took hold. What would it be lik
to be a mother? What would it be like to have someone t
call her own? An overwhelming, almost primitive desire o
longing swept through her.

"You've made a friend, I see." Dina looked up to see th
approving glint in Gabe's eyes as he slid into the vacant chai
on the other side of Dina. The rest of the family had va

ated the dining room. The sound of television cartoons merged from the living room.

"I don't think Dina had any choice," Susan said. "Samantha decided to take the first step, and your niece has a mind of her own."

Gabe leaned towards Samantha. She reached for his nose. He caught her arm and rubbed his whiskers gently across it. Samantha giggled, still managing to keep her finger stuck in her mouth.

"It looks like someone is getting sleepy," Susan observed. "Can you watch her while I go get her bottle ready, Dina?"

After Susan left, Gabe continued his private conversation with his niece. Dina noticed the contrast of Gabe's dark head and the fair-haired baby. The big man and the small child. They seemed to be experiencing no trouble bridging the generation gap.

Gabe anchored his arm along the back of Dina's chair. "You have a natural way with children."

Dina's lips turned into a self-mocking grimace. "She's smiling now. I'd probably jump into the river if she started crying."

Gabe shook his head. "I don't believe that for a minute."

She chewed nervously on her lip. In actuality, she could readily picture a sturdy toddler with Gabe's personality and her red hair.

Dangerous thoughts, an inner voice warned her. But how could she resist the temptation to dream with Samantha nestled against her breast? She turned her eyes away from the baby and caught Gabe's intent stare. It was personal and very intimate. She tried to look away but found she couldn't.

Gabe brushed his thumb against her cheek. "It's a wonderful thing when two people can create such a beautiful reflection of themselves." His voice was deep and penetrating.

Dina fought the pull he had on her. He wasn't playing fair. His steady gaze demanded she explore the possibili-

ties. She couldn't seem to break through the seductive spell
he wove around her. Fresh air was in short supply, and her
fantasies were stronger and more vivid now. Couples. Family togetherness. Sweet-smelling babies. How much more of
this intimacy could she take?

"You miss so much of her growing up by living here,
don't you? How can you stand it?" she asked, almost desperately.

"I do miss her. She's grown at least two inches in the past
two months."

Naomi overheard them. "That's why you need to come
home for a visit." She leaned across the table and gathered
up the mugs, twisted napkins and sticky spoons. "Why
don't you bring Dina and Wally to Quarry City for Christmas?"

"I'll let you know, Mom" was Gabe's noncommittal answer to his mother although his gaze met Dina's.

Dina wanted to ignore the unspoken questions in Gabe's
eyes. She felt a smothering closeness descend around her.
Thanksgiving...then Christmas? She didn't want those
kinds of demands and ties. They could only lead to expectations and eventual heartache. On the other hand, the sight
of the child in her arms was stirring up biological urges
again. She'd been so content not knowing this desire before.

Hadn't she? So why were those desires flowing through
her as if a floodgate had been opened.

Susan returned to the dining room. "Since you're holding her, Dina, do you want to help me put her to bed?"

Trying not to jostle the dozing child, Dina rose to her feet
carefully and followed Susan out of the room. After laying
Samantha down in her travel bed, she forced herself to leave
the room without a backward glance.

She didn't feel ready to face the masses again. She slipped
into her own bedroom and closed the door. Sitting on the
bed, her arms feeling strangely light and useless, she already missed the baby's warm body pressed against hers.

Get a grip, she ordered herself. *You don't want that kind
of responsibility, that kind of stress. What if something*

happened and you couldn't save your own child? You couldn't even save your own husband or your marriage. You'd never be able to cope if something happened to your child.

But the argument in her head didn't stand a chance against Samantha's scent, which still lingered on her shirt, or the memories of the baby's smile, her jabbering speech, or her warm softness. Try as she might, Dina couldn't banish the fierce longing to hold a baby to her breast. Lord, her arms felt like empty appendages, hanging useless at her sides. And she couldn't forget the steady pressure of Gabe's eyes. The expectations. The need. She cursed him for making her feel things she shouldn't be feeling.

She wasn't even remotely qualified to be a parent. It wasn't enough just to want a child or even a happy marriage. Brenda and Susan had nurturing backgrounds that had no doubt prepared them to be supportive wives and wonderful parents.

Dina hadn't had that kind of upbringing. She'd had a grandfather who was loving but who would have preferred a grandson instead of a granddaughter; an aunt who had embraced an independent life-style and scorned wedlock; and a workaholic husband who didn't like children. What kind of background was that for family life?

The odds were stacked against her.

So why did her womb seem so painfully vacant all of a sudden?

The murmured sounds of conversation, laughter and an occasional thump indicated that the Randolph family was moving about the house. Tomorrow at this time they would be gone, and Dina didn't know how she was going to stand the silence they would leave behind.

Would she ever see any of them again? It was doubtful. By Christmas, Gabe would have moved into his apartment above the restaurant. Dina would have the farm pretty much to herself with only Aunt Wally for company. And who knew when the traveling bug would take her aunt to some forgotten corner of the world?

Then Dina would be on her own.

Alone again. Just the way she liked it.

Or the way she used to like it.

Would she ever again be able to appreciate her independent way of life?

She would be reinstated as a fire fighter, of course.

But the thought gave her no comfort.

A knock sounded on the door. When she opened it, she expected to see Gabe but discovered Naomi instead.

Naomi gave her a tentative smile. "I hate to disturb you Dina, but I thought maybe we could have a moment to chat without any interruptions."

Dina moved back to allow the older woman to step into her room. "Come on in. I didn't intend to be antisocial. was just taking a short break."

"You don't have to apologize to me. I've spent half my life trying to find a quiet moment." Naomi walked over and sat down in the wicker chair next to the bed, while Dina returned to her spot on the mattress.

"You have a wonderful family," Dina told the older woman with genuine sincerity.

"Yes, I do. And they certainly make life interesting sometimes. Parents never quite know what's going to be thrown at them." Naomi's eyes filled with moisture.

A wave of sympathy swept through Dina. She leaned across and rested a hand on Naomi's tightly folded hands. "This must be a tough holiday to face without Danny."

Naomi blinked and regained her composure. "Things will never be quite the same without him. He was always the life of the party. We miss him." Naomi sighed, and Dina didn't interrupt with a meaningless platitude. Gabe's mother obviously needed to talk. The older woman continued, "We never would have pulled together as a family if it wasn't for Gabriel. We've always looked to him for strength and stability."

Dina could understand how the family found it so easy to lean on Gabe. There was a strength to him that invited a sense of security. "He's a strong man."

Naomi nodded. "Yes, he is. But Daniel's death was probably a bigger blow to Gabriel than to any of us. Ga briel and Daniel were close when they were growing up, but they were as different as day and night. They had contrasting philosophies about life. When Daniel died, Gabriel blamed himself because he believed his overprotectiveness drove Daniel away." Her smile bore a lingering sadness. "It wasn't true, of course. Daniel had to follow his own dreams, and I think Gabriel is finally starting to understand that. I'm so relieved to see him happy again."

Dina reached over again and squeezed Naomi's hands with understanding and comfort. "He's been able to build something positive by opening the restaurant."

Naomi shook her head "It's not the restaurant that's brought the light back to his eyes. It's you. I want to thank you, Dina, for making Gabriel happy again."

Dina stiffened with denial and tried to pull back. "I didn't have anything to do with helping Gabe," she said.

Naomi's smile widened with understanding. "You've made Gabriel trust his instincts again. He believes in himself, and he's looking toward the future."

"No, you don't understand. We—"

Naomi interrupted gently. "I know Gabriel is domineering and overly protective. It's hard for a man with his strengths to step back and accept someone else's decisions in determining his or her own life. Please give him time. As hard as it was for him to accept, he knew he was right to let Daniel leave the nest and strike out on his own." Her hands tightened around Dina's once more and then relaxed. "Now I'm going to be a foolish woman and tell you I have one more selfish wish. I hope you're part of Gabriel's future. You are a beautiful, warm person, and I would be so proud to have you in my family."

Words of denial rose to Dina's lips. She didn't want to hurt Naomi. But it was obvious Naomi was looking for a daughter-in-law. She didn't understand that Dina could never be like Brenda or Susan. She tried to temper her words, while trying to thrust back the claustrophobic panic. "I'm afraid you've misunderstood our relationship. We're merely friends."

"Friendship is the best place to start." Naomi patted her hand and rose to her feet. "I'm not trying to put any pressure on you, dear, but I had to say my piece. I hope you'll give it some thought."

Helplessly, Dina sat on the bed and watched her leave. She didn't want to believe that she'd been instrumental in producing any kind of change in Gabe. Being responsible for his contentment placed her in an increasingly vulnerable position. She didn't want to hurt Gabe or his family.

But neither did she want to love and lose again.

Outside, the wind howled. Dina shivered and tried to stifle her panic. What had she done? She'd built false hopes in a nice woman and her family. The Randolphs were the forever kind of people. They'd expect wedding bells, family reunions and baby showers.

A bell of dread tolled inside the back of her head. How had life become so complicated? How was she going to fix it?

Staring at the four walls in her bedroom wasn't providing a solution. Suddenly her immediate isolation bothered her. She left the bedroom, seeking to bury herself in the crowd so she wouldn't be able to think.

An obscenely bright sun slithered over the horizon the next morning. By midday the big snowplows had cut swaths through the white drifts blocking the roads. Gabe managed to coax the old tractor into starting, and he cleared out the snow-choked driveway. Kyle and Edward applied shovels to the sidewalk and ice scrapers to the windows of the two vehicles they were traveling home in.

After lunch and a final check with the weather service, the Randolphs loaded their possessions into the warmed-up vehicles. Unrestrained kisses and hugs were liberally given and returned. To invitations for Wally and Dina to visit the Randolphs, Dina responded with a noncommittal smile. Her cheeks ached from the effort of keeping the chiseled smile in place until the last of Gabe's family wheeled out of the farmyard.

Gabe followed his family down the road in his pickup. He planned to catch up on work at the restaurant, and he wouldn't be back until late that night.

Dina headed straight for her isolated workroom for a few hours of work.

Later that afternoon, she received a phone call from JD.

"Billy Bob's been arrested and charged with starting several fires," he said.

"Has he confessed to the Sherman fires?" she asked.

JD sighed. "Not yet. The investigators have an airtight case for two of the fires. It should be just a matter of time before they break him down, and he gives a full confession."

"Then it's over?"

"It looks that way. Welcome back to the department, honey" were JD's parting words.

That evening following a meal of leftovers with Aunt Wally, the older woman prodded Dina into playing a game of gin rummy. After the cards had been dealt, Wally said, "I talked to the mayor today and he told me Essie Mae has been under sedation since Billy Bob's arrest."

"I'm sure it's a shock," Dina said, trying to keep up with her aunt's interesting card moves.

"It's kind of quiet around here, isn't it?"

Dina looked at her aunt in surprise. "It's always been quiet."

"Yes, but there are different degrees of quiet. This kind of quiet is almost unnatural in a big house. The other quiet is that internal contentment you share with a family at the end of the day. Didn't you hear it last night after everyone was asleep? There was a rewarding peacefulness, knowing everyone was tucked in safe and sound. A rich kind of contentment. You noticed it, didn't you?" Her aunt was watching her closely.

Dina decided that her best course of action was to hedge. "It was nice. I enjoyed having the Randolphs here. But they had to go home sometime."

"I suppose Gabriel will be moving back into town pretty soon."

Dina swallowed and clutched her cards tightly but without really seeing them. "Yes, I suppose he will."

Wally casually laid out a run of threes. "You could ask Gabriel to stay and start working on a new kind of quiet." Her aunt plunked down her final cards and stood up. "Wouldn't that be nice to have a real family for a change?"

Dina shook her head then realized her aunt had already left the room. It was just as well. She couldn't tell her the truth that she was scared to death to let Gabe stay. If he stayed, they'd get more involved. Her defenses against him were nearly in shambles already.

In asking Gabe to stay, she'd be facing a lifetime of uncertainties. She'd have to risk her heart and emotional security again. She knew she didn't have that kind of strength or fortitude. She'd lost too many times, and had barely recouped her emotional resources.

The poignant memory of baby Samantha surfaced. Dina's heart squeezed painfully. A basic fundamental need to take a chance on love again battled with the painful facts of reality. If only she had the courage to follow her heart and desires.

The evening slipped away, and Dina went to bed only to find herself wide awake. Why couldn't life be simpler? Why couldn't it be like the fairy tales where you knew everyone lived happily ever after?

No pain.

No loss.

No fear of falling in love.

She sensed Gabe was falling in love with her. It was there in the possessive gleam in his eyes.

She knew she was falling in love with him. But could she risk loving him?

The thought of such a commitment scared the hell out of her. But would life be worth living without him?

The next morning, Gabe showed up in the kitchen while she was midway through breakfast. He handed her a familiar-looking photo album. "I found this on your bookshelf.

You've met my family, so how about if you introduce me to the rest of yours?''

She hesitated, and then used her finger to trace the gold lettering on the old brown cover. The scent of leather wafted through the air, and Dina's appetite fled. She'd kept the album buried under her socks and underwear for the past three years. Two days ago she'd dug it out, but she hadn't been ready to explore the pages. Was she prepared to look into faces of her loved ones again? She missed them all so much. What memories and emotions would be unleashed? Did she want to share them with Gabe?

He didn't pressure her, but watched and waited for her to decide.

She cleared the hoarseness from her voice and said, ''Pull up a chair.''

Several times during the next hour, tears rose to her eyes. But they were good tears. Happy tears.

Gabe pointed to a picture of her as a little girl. ''This looks like the feed store. Are you standing next to your grandfather?''

She nodded. ''The roof needed some maintenance and Gramps did the work. I was always with him at the construction sites, so when the guy from the newspaper took the picture, I was in it, too. I was the most popular girl in school for a whole week. I wouldn't let anyone forget my celebrity status, either.''

The memories made her feel good inside. She'd buried those remembrances for a long time. Sharing them with Gabe now was a cleansing, insightful experience.

Suddenly Gabe leaned over and kissed her sweetly on the mouth. The tingles started in her toes and raced to the tips of her breasts. Before she could loop her hands behind his head and deepen the kiss, Gabe pulled back. ''I think you'd better turn the page, honey, or neither of us will get anything done for the rest of the day.''

She couldn't deny the disappointment tugging at her emotions. Why did the world always slant silly when he kissed her? She met his gaze, feeling elated but a bit wary at the same time. ''Why did you kiss me?''

"Because I wanted to share your happiness." Then he leaned over and closed the book. There was a finality and sense of closure in his action. Gabe stood up and set the album on the counter. Then he turned back toward her but stayed where he was. His expression was set as if he had something distasteful on his mind. "We need to talk."

She braced herself. "All right."

"I'm moving back into town today," he said grimly.

Her throat tightened. She knew this moment was coming, but she still wasn't prepared for it. She tilted her chin with a bravery she didn't feel. "Where will you go?"

His jaw clenched when he realized she wasn't going to argue with him. "I'm going to move into the apartment above the restaurant."

Despite her logical brain telling her this was for the best, she floundered, searching for a reason to stall the inevitable. "Has the fire captain inspected it yet?"

"He's stopping by sometime this week."

"Maybe you should wait until he's checked everything out."

Gabe shook his head, his gaze never breaking its lock on hers. "I need to leave before I do something we'll both regret."

A sliver of longing cut through her. "And what is that?" she whispered.

"Walk through your bedroom door and make love to you," he said with an intensity that told her he meant every word.

She tried to swallow the hard lump in her throat, while wishing he would do exactly that very thing. She didn't want him to leave. "Would that be so awful?"

"No. I suspect it would be heaven on earth," he said with painful honesty. "But I couldn't make love to you and have you kick me out the door later. And you would eventually kick me out, wouldn't you, Dina? Especially when you realize what I really want."

She managed a tight smile, but she wondered if her heart had ever hurt so badly. "What exactly do you want?" Her voice was barely a whisper.

"I want what your husband had." He walked across the room and pulled her from her chair. "In fact, I want more than he had." His gaze was relentless. Then his hands came down on her shoulders, and she could feel them tremble, giving testimony to his desire to hold her. "I want a promise for the future. I want you as my wife."

She squeezed her eyes shut, trying to ward off the pain of futility. It was hopeless. Somehow she found the strength to pull herself out of his arms. "I never promised you any of that." The lump grew in the back of her throat, making talking difficult, but she forged ahead anyway. "Life doesn't always give us a choice. You know that as well as I do. I screwed up once. I'm not sure I can handle that responsibility again."

"Ask me to stay, and we'll work through it together." His tone was almost hypnotic in its urgency.

"Ask?" Her laugh sounded more like a whimper of pain. "That sounded more like a demand."

"In your heart, you know it's what we both want."

"You can't know what I want or need. Nobody can." She knew her words were hurting both of them. But she also knew they had to be said for both of their sakes.

He cut her no slack. "Tell me what you felt when you kissed me."

Why was he doing this to her? Why was he pressuring her? "You know what I felt."

"Uncertain. Needy. Crazy. Out of control." His voice was compelling, revealing the power of his own emotions.

It was almost her undoing. She wanted to put her hands over her ears and block out his words. But she didn't. "I don't think this discussion is relevant."

He refused to let her escape. "Did you want it to end, Dina?"

"I didn't!" she shouted at him. "Is that what you wanted to hear? I didn't want it to end *ever*."

He refused to give up. His hands bit into her shoulders. "You're no longer in charge of your safe little world when I'm around, and that scares the hell out of you, doesn't it?"

She felt like a fly stuck in wet paint—squirming and fluttering, but unable to escape. "What do you want?" she repeated almost desperately.

"Everything. I want *everything* you have to offer. I want you to give me your heart and trust me to take care of it," he vowed. His pledge seduced and beguiled her.

For a moment, she was almost hypnotized by his need for her. She wanted him, but wanting was not enough. It never had been. Love could be here today and gone tomorrow. She must never forget that. She shook her head vehemently. "You expect too much. You were raised differently than I was, Gabe. I've always taken care of myself. The only time I didn't was when I fell in love and married Jerry. His death almost destroyed me."

"But you survived," he argued earnestly. "You're a stronger person now."

She refused to hear him. "You want a woman who is like your mother. Or like Susan and Brenda. You want a woman who isn't afraid to take the risk of being a wife and mother. I can never be that woman. I've lost too many people and failed at the one relationship that meant the most to me. I can't risk that kind of failure again. I don't believe in happily-ever-after anymore."

"It exists only if two people are willing to try," Gabe pressed. If she would just give them a chance, he knew time would erase her fears. He wished he could have waited and given her more time, but he didn't think he'd last another night knowing she was only a room away from him. And physical pleasure wouldn't give him what he wanted most. He wanted it all.

Dina pulled herself from his arms and walked away from him, hoping the distance would help heal the pain throbbing between them. But it was useless. She still wanted him. "That's fantasy. Real life is unpredictable."

He let her go, his expression grim and unyielding. "Is that what you want? Predictability?" He crossed his arms, looking as unmovable as the bluffs along the river. "I'm not safe enough like your good buddy, Ralph, am I? I suppose I should be thankful for that small compliment. But is that how you want to live your life, Dina? No sparks? No surprises?"

"At least I know what's coming," she pleaded for understanding. Her head started to pound, and a tear escaped the corner of her eye. Life wasn't being fair. Why couldn't things be perfect? "Jerry and I knew each other inside out. We were best friends but couldn't fulfill each other. I thought children might fill the void, while Jerry tried to make his job fill his. We failed to make our marriage work. There are no certainties. Promises of forever can be broken even if you don't want them to." She paused and waited for the understanding to dawn in Gabe's eyes. When it didn't happen, she added, "Don't you see, I just can't stand the uncertainty of waiting for Fate's other shoe to fall. I'd be waiting for you to be as disappointed as Jerry was. Jerry *knew* me, but in the end it wasn't enough."

In so many ways, she'd already given more of herself to Gabe than she'd ever given to Jerry. With Jerry, she'd had no barriers. They'd fallen in love as a matter of course, following a lifetime friendship. With Gabe, it was different. She'd blocked him at every corner and still he'd scaled the walls with an ease that had left her reeling and yearning.

Gabe had made her aware of the true depths of her passion. He'd made her hungry. He'd made her wish she could believe in the future. But she couldn't. She begged him, "I can't lose control of my life again."

In two strides, he covered the distance separating them. She found herself enfolded in his arms, his mouth pressed desperately to hers. He kissed her thoroughly, roughly, dragging the need from her and matching it with his. His desire and desperation mirrored hers. They touched each other's body and soul. She felt his frustration, his demanding need. And it scared her to death.

She pulled herself from his arms with her last ounce of strength. Her hands trembled; her head hurt.

"And how do you plan to control this?" He was hoarse, his eyes revealing the depth of his frustration. "We both are involved. Why can't you admit it?"

She shook her head. As he took a step toward her again, she held out her hand, silently begging him not to destroy what little control she had left. "I'm not the woman for you, Gabe. You're lucky to have the support of your wonderful family. But I've always walked alone."

"You don't have to do that anymore. I'll be there."

"No."

"Why? Tell me why, dammit."

Her thin rein of control snapped. The anguish poured from her soul. "Because if we failed to make this relationship work, I'd never be able to put myself back together again! I can't afford to love you. Not now. Not ever."

She never heard him leave. But she knew he had.

How was it possible that her heart could still beat inside her chest when it had just broken in two?

Chapter Nine

Stupid, stupid, stupid. She should have known better than to trust Billy Bob. He had to go and get himself caught on national television. He never did have a great deal of smarts—not like she did. Why was she the only smart person left in the world? It was because she knew how to stay in the shadows, how to bide her time, and how to get even.

She could only hope Billy Bob kept his mouth shut.

She looked out the window and checked the street furtively. Was anyone watching the house? Did they suspect her?

She'd gone too far to quit now. She wanted her revenge. She wanted her worth recognized. She was tired of living in the shadows and being the doormat everyone walked on. She was tired of playing second fiddle to another. It wasn't fair that Mother Nature and the town discriminated against brains. If only she were young again. If only she were pretty. She would have had the power long before now.

There was no way she could quit.

She'd have to plan one final fire. A fire to end all fires. She'd up the stakes. This time it couldn't be a deserted building—she'd run out of those anyway. She'd torch a building that would break the town's back—and destroy Dina Paxton forever.

Then her rival for power would be truly ousted.

She knew the perfect building. A delicious spiral of excitement swirled through her.

This time, she'd fix Dina Paxton but good. Then the town would look to her to put them back together again.

Damn him! Why couldn't she get him out of her house, her head or her heart? Dina thought to herself with a heavy dose of resignation. Another long day stretched interminably ahead of her. Somehow she'd have to get through it.

Just as the arsonist had changed forever the appearance of Sherman's downtown, Gabe had evoked similar havoc within Dina. He'd forever changed her life, and now her world had the same appeal as those desolate ashes.

She couldn't forget him. He'd left his mark. When she'd accidentally picked up a bar of his musk soap while taking a shower, she found his scent slathered all over her body. A wave of loneliness washed through her.

She avoided driving into town, fearing she'd run into him. The pain of seeing him would be almost as unbearable as the agony of not seeing him. Retrieving and hauling the crocks would have provided a physical outlet, which might have taken her mind off her moping, but Gabe had managed to bring up the rest of her supply of crocks from the shed before he left. She cursed him for that.

She couldn't stand her own company any longer so she left the workroom and found Wally in the kitchen.

"Oh good, you can join me for lunch," Wally said.

Dina grimaced at the thought of food—especially her aunt's food. "I'm not very hungry."

"Sit down anyway. We need to talk."

Dina sat down at the table and stared at a brown mushy thing sitting in the middle of the plate Wally had shoved toward her. Dina stifled a shudder and shoved it with her fork over to the rim of her plate. She couldn't rake up as much enthusiasm as she used to for Aunt Wally's cooking. Just another thing Gabe had ruined for her.

"So you let Gabriel leave?" her aunt said with disapproving tartness.

Dina sighed, not wanting to relive the scene that never seemed far from her thoughts no matter how hard she tried not to think about it. "It was his decision to leave."

"He'd have stayed if you asked him."

Dina shook her head slowly. If only it could have been that easy. "Not without a wedding ring."

"Wedding rings aren't nooses."

Dina looked pointedly to her aunt's ringless hand. "I don't see one on your finger."

Wally responded by waving her fork in the air. "Blink, and you just might."

Dina rolled her eyes in disbelief. That would be the day. "I don't blink that slowly."

"Pay attention," her aunt said irritably, causing Dina to look up. "I'm getting married."

Dina refused to take her seriously. "Are you pregnant?"

Wally scowled as she helped herself to another generous scoop of a mysterious salad. "My ovaries retired years ago, and JD already had a son."

Dina's fork dropped to her plate. Her mouth opened, and then shut. She couldn't believe she'd heard her aunt correctly. "You're marrying JD? You're joking."

Her aunt frowned. "I've never joked about marriage in my life. Marriage is a serious step for a woman—even an old woman."

Dina stared at her aunt. Concern replaced surprise. Was her aunt sick? No, she couldn't be. The sharpness, clearness and shrewdness were still there in her aunt's eyes. But so was a light of happiness. Dina shook her head in wonder. "You really are getting married, aren't you?"

"Does that bother you?" Wally asked softly, her eyes pleading for understanding and acceptance.

Dina, still trying to deal with the shock, didn't know how to respond. "I'm not sure. When did this happen?"

Wally set down her own fork and placed a hand over Dina's. "I've been given a second chance for love, and this time I'm smart enough to grab it and hang on."

"A second chance?"

Wally settled in her chair and folded her hands in an un-Wally-like manner. She appeared to be bracing herself for an unpleasant task. "I fell in love thirty years ago at a peace demonstration in Washington, D.C., when I marched alongside a wild-haired member of the clergy, who had great idealistic plans for changing the ways of our selfish society. He wanted to get married. But marriage was not in my plans. Freedom was my battle cry. I didn't want to tie my-self to babies or a kitchen like other women my age. Mar-riage symbolized bondage, and I wanted no part of it. Besides, it wouldn't have worked. Can you imagine me be-ing a minister's wife, leading the Sunday choir?"

In Dina's mind, it was harder to imagine her aunt in love once, let alone twice. Wally had always been so proud of her independence. Dina picked up the saltshaker and rolled it between her palms. "You've had a wonderful life. You've enjoyed your independence."

"Sure I have," Wally said with a grimace. "I pursued my career and lived with the knowledge that the man I loved married a woman who wasn't afraid to share his life and have his babies."

Fear was not a word Dina associated with her aunt, but then neither was marriage. "But you've been happy."

"In one sense, I was," Wally agreed. Then her expres-sion turned wistful. "My life was everything I thought it should be, but my heart never fully agreed. Friends and commitments can be as lonely as an empty motel room if you don't have someone special to love or someone special to love you."

Dina didn't think she'd ever hear such a speech from her aunt. It confused her because she always considered Wally the one constant in her life. Now she wasn't sure what to believe anymore. "Why didn't you tell me this before?"

"I never have been one to dwell on my past mistakes. It's redundant, and I could never take back what I'd already done." A sheepish expression slid across Wally's face be-fore she continued, "I also didn't want to fall off the ped-estal you'd put me on. I was afraid to let you see all my wrinkles and scars. You were the daughter I never allowed myself to have. I needed your hero worship, and I was too insecure to jeopardize the relationship we had.''

Dina struggled to fit Wally's revelations with the Aunt Wally she thought she knew and remembered. They didn't match. "You were like a fairy godmother. Your visits made my life exciting and so much fun. How can you apologize for that?''

Wally gave her a droll look. "Have you ever noticed that fairy godmothers only show up when they choose? They're rather selfish creatures.''

Dina gave her aunt a long, considering look, trying to interpret the meanings and hidden truths. "Why are you telling me this now?''

"Because I don't want you to make the same mistake I did in thinking work and friends are enough to give your life meaning. I don't want you to wake up some morning thirty years from now and realize you gave up love and married loneliness instead. I lived with that knowledge for almost thirty years. Don't make the same mistake I did, honey.'' Wally reached over and took the saltshaker from Dina's limp fingers. "Life comes with no money-back guarantees. Do you regret loving Jerry?''

"Of course not!'' She and Jerry had made mistakes but she would always carry in her heart the memories of what they'd shared during the good times.

"Do you love Gabriel?'' Wally posed the question that had been haunting Dina ever since Gabe had walked out the door.

Dina's fingers tucked into taut fists. She couldn't deny it. "Love isn't enough.''

"Honey, does Gabriel visit your dreams every night?''

Dina's flush gave her away.

Wally planted her hands on the table and gave Dina an admonishing look such as a parent would give an obtuse child. "I can tell you from too many years of experience, he'll still be visiting your dreams fifty years from now. Those dreams are nothing but mist and vapor next to the solid warmth of the real man. You might find it takes more strength to live without him than to live with him."

The doorbell rang, and Dina pondered her aunt's words as Wally let JD into the house. Dina stood up and walked into her father-in-law's arms and gave him a big hug. "Congratulations," she said, giving him a warm smile that reflected all the love she had for this dear man.

He hugged her back, then regarded her with shrewd but loving eyes. "You don't mind?"

"Mind that the two people I love so dearly have found happiness together?" She shook her head. "I'm thrilled. But I can't believe I didn't notice what was going on."

"You had a lot on your mind. We all did," he reminded her.

He released her and reached over to give Wally a sound kiss. Dina watched with amusement as her usually unshakable aunt blushed. JD pulled Wally down next to him on the couch, his arm anchoring her to his side. Wally's glow gave Dina comfort. Her aunt deserved to be happy. Maybe marriage was the right step for Wally after all.

And what about marriage for you? her heart asked.

Dina ignored her heart's yearnings. "When are you getting married?"

"We haven't set a date," Wally answered. Her eyes darted to JD's. "We'd like to see you settled."

"Settled?"

"What your aunt means if we'd like to see you kiss and make up with Gabe first," JD said.

Dina's gaze narrowed as certain things began to make sense—such as JD's arranging for Gabe to live at the farm. "Have you two been playing matchmaker?"

JD had the audacity to wink at her. "Cupid can always use a little assistance."

"We just want you to be happy, dear," Wally added.

Dina couldn't be angry with either of them. Whatever they'd done, they'd done it because they loved her. "I love you both, but I'm not going to plan my future to accommodate you. This is your moment. Enjoy it. I'll be fine."

Wally and JD exchanged looks. After which Wally said, 'We love you, honey. You do what's best for you and you'll have our unconditional support.''

Would she ever have the courage to take the risks her aunt had taken? Above all else, Dina feared becoming so dependent on another person again. She'd lost her parents before she even knew them. When Jerry died, the one friendship she'd relied on through the years disappeared. She was afraid if she formed a relationship with Gabe, she'd always be looking over her shoulder, worrying that something would drive him away.

But looking at the happiness in front of her, she craved the emotional satisfaction her aunt and JD were experiencing.

The telephone rang. It was a call for JD.

Left alone with her aunt, Dina regarded her with loving affection. "You needn't worry."

"About what?"

"Your pedestal is solidly in place, Aunt Wally." Then she gave her aunt a warm hug and returned to her solitary workroom.

In the wake of her aunt's happiness, her own restlessness increased by leaps and bounds, and a new sense of dissatisfaction manifested itself. How could she face another endless night without Gabe? Or a lifetime?

He was tired to the bone, Gabe thought as he locked up the restaurant and climbed the narrow stairs to his small apartment at the top and rear of the building. Weariness dragged at his heels. He hated the claustrophobic atmosphere. The apartment had only one window, which provided a picturesque view of the bank's brick wall only four feet away, and the fire inspector had warned him that the narrow fire escape outside the window was dangerous and should be replaced.

He'd been living out of a suitcase, unwilling to acknowledge, even in a small way, that he wasn't going to be invited back to Dina's. He should probably check around for a small house to rent or to buy. Someplace he could call home, and where he could move more than eight feet in one direc tion. Right now, he'd settle for ten more feet of pacing room. How had he ever thought he could live in this tiny box?

He sighed. Who was he trying to kid? He didn't want to live anywhere that didn't have Dina.

Had he ever spent a more miserable night? Hell, the last few nights had been awful. He hadn't slept, and he was exhausted. For his own sanity, he'd tried not to think about Dina. The minute he closed his eyes, however, all he could see was a pert, freckled nose, intelligent green eyes and a wide, kissable mouth. So his eyes stayed open, never relaxing their guard. How much more of this could he take?

It was his own fault. He'd backed Dina into a corner. He should have known better.

Dina had his heart, and he strongly suspected he held hers. The fact she was still scared about rushing into a relationship wasn't a surprise. She'd suffered a lifetime of losses. Why hadn't he understood she'd need more than a few weeks to accept a love for the future? What a pompous ass he'd been! He'd patronized her vulnerability instead of supporting her and giving her the time she needed. She didn't have to be on his timetable.

She did love him, he was sure of it. She responded to him on every level—emotionally, physically and spiritually— whether she wanted to admit it or not. But he'd rushed her, demanded she commit her heart on his terms.

There was no other woman for him than Dina. He didn't want to contemplate the future without her. It wasn't worth even thinking about. But wasn't that exactly what he was afraid would happen?

He stood up and paced.

For the first time, he tunneled through his own darkness, seeking the home truths he'd previously avoided. He knew he loved Dina. *But did he love her enough to risk losing her?*

The pain ripped through him. The hurt inside his chest swelled and overflowed.

The danger from the arsonist appeared to be over, but Dina's fire fighting scared him, made him uncomfortably vulnerable. She was dedicated to helping others—just as Danny had been—and that made her a target for getting hurt or worse. He couldn't forget seeing her burst through the door of the feed store, the flames licking at her heels. How could he protect her when she was in a blazing building? Even if there was never another fire like the three that had almost destroyed Sherman, Dina could die in a car accident. She could fall down the basement steps. She could be electrocuted in the bathroom. The possibilities immobilized him. He might not be able to protect her just as he hadn't been able to protect his brother from being himself.

He'd lost Danny. But he couldn't imagine his brother ever finding fulfillment in his life if he'd had to be less than what he was. Gabe could never regret that Danny had followed his own dreams.

He couldn't demand that of Dina, either. The question was whether or not he could live with the fear of losing her. Would he become too protective and try to change her? Danny had resisted Gabe's overprotectiveness. Dina would, too.

The other option was to live without her.

Forget it, a voice in the back of his head said flatly. With every last breath he took, he'd always love her. Always need her.

What was life without Dina?

Could he be less of a man so she could be more of a woman? Or could they both be strong and learn to accept each other for who they were?

He wanted to be with her now. *Don't put it off, Gabriel. Go to her now,* the nagging inner voice urged.

No, he couldn't do it—not until he knew he could give her what she needed: his trust in allowing her to be Dina and everything she was. He wasn't sure he could do that.

The inner battle wore him down as the sleepless nights took their toll. His eyes drifted shut.

Was Gabe sleeping? Dina wondered at one-thirty in the morning as she plopped down on the couch for the umpteenth time. Her body was tight with unreleased tensions.

Why was this night so long? Why was she fighting such a strong sense of urgency?

She heard each tick of the hall clock and still she couldn't relax.

Something had to give. She couldn't go through life as she had the past few days—fearing Gabe would come to her, fearing he wouldn't. She'd briefly toyed with the idea of calling Ralph and asking him if he wanted to go to a movie. She'd banished the idea as quickly as it popped into her head. Socializing with Ralph for an entire lifetime couldn't be as fulfilling as spending one hour with Gabe. With Gabe, she felt complete, part of a whole. When she was with anyone else, she was incomplete—and still alone.

Why was she dithering?

Gabe didn't fit into the background of her life. He also didn't need to be compared to Jerry at every turn. She and Jerry had been young—no more than children when they'd married. They'd grown up during their marriage, but in different directions. Gabe wasn't a child. He was a man. A man who knew what he wanted. Why was she trying to paint him with the same brush as Jerry?

She loved Gabe, but was she strong enough to make a lifetime commitment? That was what she had to decide: all or nothing. With Gabe, she couldn't hold back and keep herself protected against future hurts. He wouldn't allow it.

She rolled over onto her side, thinking about Wally and JD's newly found contentment. Her aunt, whom she considered to be a shrewd woman, had lived a remarkable, adventuresome life. Who would have guessed underneath all the tart comments was a heart still yearning? Seeing the love in Wally's face when JD walked through the door was an incredible experience. It was like watching a baby take its first step. Newness. Joy. Even uncertainty. Would that baby fall? And if it did, would it have the courage to get back up again?

Her aunt had quit fighting her own ghosts and was now ready to face the future. Why couldn't Dina?

Did she want some other woman to have Gabe's children?

The torment of such a thought nearly ripped out her heart.

He's mine!

She tossed aside the blanket.

She couldn't pretend to sleep. Energy churned within her.

Don't wait. Go to Gabe now, the insistent voice inside her head demanded.

I can't! the other voice inside her stated with absolute certainty. She couldn't go to Gabe half a woman. He deserved more from a wife and a lifetime partner than a coward. She had to be sure.

She stood looking around the room, agitation whipping her emotions. What could she do to combat this endless quiet? The carpet would be worn thin by morning if she started to pace. Her body craved action; her mind wanted satisfaction. Her gaze landed on the string of pictures across the room. She knew what she had to do. It was time to put the past to rest.

Carefully she took down each framed photo of Jerry. Then she spent the next hour transferring the photographs into the family album. Satisfaction rolled through her after she completed that task.

Then she headed to her workroom.

From its isolated shelf, she retrieved the uncompleted fire-painted crock and went to work. She scraped the vicious slashes of orange, red and yellow, taming them into a single spark. Then she applied her paintbrush and drew a brown match stem across the surface. When she was finished, she held a container that could be used for matches and set on a fireplace mantel safely out of a child's reach. Pleasure glowed within her as she looked down at her handiwork. She had taken another step in claiming the future.

But it still wasn't enough.

Sighing, she cleaned her brushes and was turning off the workroom light, when the fire call came from the dispatcher.

"Fire at Dare'n Gabe's Restaurant."

No! For a moment, the room spun crazily. It couldn't be. *Gabe was there.*

She didn't remember driving to the fire station. She didn't recall donning her gear. All she knew was the fear charging through her.

Not now. I won't lose him now ran the chant in her head as she raced with the other fire fighters toward the billowing smoke that was choking the street and covering the restaurant.

Pain squeezed her heart. She realized now that nothing had prepared her for losing Gabe—or ever would. How could she have been such a fool to let him go?

Chapter Ten

"Is anyone in there?" one of the fire fighters yelled as the others moved quickly to connect the hose to the town's water supply.

"The fire's blocking those back stairs!"

"Where's Gabe?" Dina shouted. She searched the building's windows for any signs of life. The darkness of the night made it difficult to see into the shadows of the restaurant. The smoke thickened, and although she couldn't see the flames, she knew they would soon flare to life. Terror shot through her. She remembered all too clearly the ferocity and wanton destruction from the earlier fires. Those fires had shown no mercy. They had been the works of a force far beyond the volunteers' control.

Her panic increased. "Has anyone seen Gabe Randolph?"

"Haven't seen him" came the answer.

Was he already dead? She refused to consider such a thought.

"Damn!" JD cursed as he eyed the only window pinned between the two buildings. "We can't get a ladder in there."

"I'll take the fire escape." Dina started forward.

JD grabbed her arm. ''No, that fire escape is rotted. It would collapse under your weight.''

She tugged on her arm. ''I'm light.''

''Listen to me, Dina. You can't save him if you're buried in the rubble. You'll have to go in from the roof.''

His words penetrated the fog of fear. He was right. She'd have to keep her head clear. Gabe needed her levelheadedness not her hysteria. ''Okay, get me on the roof. I'll lower myself into the window.''

Precious seconds ticked away as she was raised to the roof. Her heartbeat hammered sickeningly inside her chest. She struggled to keep her mind focused and off her increasing dread as she prayed for guidance. For luck. For Gabe's life. She focused her thoughts on Gabe.

Why hadn't he heard the trucks? The apartment was way to the back of the building, but surely it wasn't sound-proof. *Please, God, don't take Gabe, too.* As soon as she hit the roof, she was off and running to the far corner. Two other fire fighters raced with her. At the edge of the roof, they worked together to attach the kernmantle rope around her.

''Dina, take it easy when you hit that fire escape.'' The warning came from above as she was lowered down. ''It's flimsy. Don't take any chances. We'll get him out another way if we can't get to him here.''

She had to reach Gabe. There wasn't another way out. She just hoped she was in time. She refused to think about what she'd do if she wasn't. Gabe Randolph was hers, and she wasn't going to hand him over to Death. She saw her future more clearly through the rolling blackness than she had ever before. And Gabe was definitely part of it.

She wasn't twenty-five and trapped by an unfulfilling life. She had a successful business and she enjoyed her fire fighting. Her external life was good. The only emptiness was the space in her heart. Only Gabe could fill the vacuum.

She couldn't lose him. She wouldn't.

''Hurry!'' she shouted to the men above.

She wanted to share a lifetime with Gabe, not face a life-time of lonely, meaningless regrets.

Sweat trickled along her jaw as she slid down the brick wall. The descent seemed painfully slow. "Hurry up!" she yelled again at the other fire fighters. She only had a few more feet to go and then she'd be there.

"Wait a minute, Dina. We've hit a snag. Hang on a sec."

She didn't have a second! Gabe could be breathing in toxic fumes right now. For endless seconds, she dangled. So close. But not close enough.

She looked below her. Only a few feet separated her from the landing outside the window. Frantically she worked at the knot around her waist. It resisted her fumblings, but she persisted.

Then the knot was freed, and letting go of the rope, she jumped.

The moment she hit the landing, the boards beneath her feet cracked. And broke. In desperation, she lunged toward the window, grasping for the windowsill as the landing first wobbled and then collapsed below her.

Suddenly two hands grabbed and yanked her through the open space.

"What in the hell are you doing? Trying to kill yourself?" Gabe's face bore raging fury as he shook her.

Smoke poured between them. He coughed.

She thrust her oxygen mask over his face. "Breathe." Then she pointed toward the window.

When he realized she expected him to escape through the window, he shook his head violently and ripped away the mask. "Forget it," he shouted. "I don't like heights."

"The stairs are blocked! We have to use the window." Then she coughed.

Her cough terrified him. He forced the mask back over her mouth. He had to get her out of here. If they had to go through the window, so be it.

She tied the rope dangling outside the window around his waist.

"What about you?" he asked with his leg hitched over the sill. "I'm not leaving you behind."

"I'll be right behind you!" she lied.

He looked ready to argue.

She desperately needed his cooperation. "Gabe, I can't spend the next fifty years with you if we both die in here," she shouted hoarsely.

He looked stunned as if he hadn't heard her correctly. "Fifty years?"

"Go now!" She pushed.

He finally let go of the window and let the rope lower him slowly to the ground. He never looked down, but kept his eyes glued on Dina's face. The smoke swirled around her. She was yelling something at the men on the roof, but he couldn't make out the words. A knot formed in his gut as he sank farther and farther away from her. He should never have let her talk him into going first.

Then his feet hit the ground.

And Dina was suddenly gone from his sight.

"Dina!" he roared. *Where was she?*

Hands pulled him. A blanket came down over his shoulders. But he shrugged it off.

"Gabe! Come on. Move back from the building." JD suddenly arrived at his side. "Let Dina do her job. We need to get you away from here."

"What if it explodes?" Gabe asked, fear clawing his insides.

"It won't," JD assured him. "The fire's under control."

It didn't look like the fire was under control. The smoke appeared thicker, blacker. He couldn't even see the window any longer. Damn, it was dark. What if Dina took one chance too many? Where in the hell was she? He struggled to keep his sanity and his faith in Dina. This was the powerlessness he most feared.

He had to trust her. This was the test, but he didn't like it one damn bit. "Why is there so much smoke?" he asked in a raw voice.

"Probably a petroleum-based fire" was the unsatisfactory answer.

Where was Dina? Dammit, why in the hell was she risking her life for a pile of boards? The restaurant could be rebuilt. Dina wasn't replaceable. He'd blown his opportunities. He could have spent last night **at the farm** with Dina. He could have loved her from dusk until dawn, but instead he'd rushed her, demanded more than she was ready to give. If he'd stayed, they could have talked, kissed and loved each other, and gradually she would have learned to run the risk of loving again.

He'd been pompous and arrogant. If she came out of the building, he was going to haunt her footsteps for the rest of her life until she agreed to marry him.

Where in the hell was she?

Above the noise he shouted to JD, "How much air does she have left?"

JD was talking into some kind of walkie-talkie before turning to answer him. "She's wearing a thirty-minute pack."

"How long has she been in there?" It seemed like an eternity had passed instead of a matter of minutes. Gabe never took his eyes from the burning building as he followed JD.

"Dina knows what she's doing."

JD's evasiveness didn't answer his question. "Tell me. How much time does she have?"

"Possibly twenty minutes."

Possibly? To hell with it! "Give me a pack. I'm going in."

Just then, one of the fire fighters ran from the first floor of the restaurant. "Hey! We need some medical assistance right away."

Gabe charged the restaurant at a dead run. Fear released the adrenaline. He ignored the yelling behind him.

He reached the front door just as three figures emerged. Two fire fighters were supporting a small person in black. For a moment, Gabe's breath jammed in his throat. Then he realized it wasn't Dina's lifeless body in the middle.

"Gabe, move back." The voice belonged to Dina and came from the fire fighter on the left who was supporting the victim's weight.

Relief poured through him.

As soon as the small figure in black was laid down next to the medical personnel, Gabe reached for Dina. He knocked off her helmet and buried his face into her damp, curly hair.

The rapid beat of his heart pounded next to her cheek. For a moment, he just held her close. "Woman, don't ever pull another stunt like that again."

She shook her head tiredly. "You never should have been in that building. Those upstairs rooms don't meet fire code."

He lifted his head and peered down at her with an intensity she felt all the way to her toes. "Did you mean what you said? About fifty years?"

Her anger and fear slipped away. A smile began and expanded. "I might consider sixty."

"Are you saying what I think you're saying?" His voice was thick and uncertain.

"Hey, Gabe!" one of the fire fighters interrupted. "Do you happen to know why Kordelia Simpson was hiding in your storage closet?"

The small figure, dressed in black, was sitting on the ground coughing. As the light from the street lamp illuminated the familiar face, Dina pulled out of Gabe's arms and frowned. "Kordelia, what were you doing inside the restaurant?"

"You!" Kordelia glared at Dina. Her hate electrified the air. "You should be dead!"

Three hours later in the crowded sheriff's office, Dina sat next to Gabe. JD stood across the room next to the mayor and the sheriff. A dozen or so town residents were hovering in the doorway, trying to take in every word. Wally had already left because she wanted to develop her latest role on film.

Kordelia, with the promise of a shorter sentence in exchange for her testimony against Billy Bob, had finally agreed to give them a full confession about her involvement in the Sherman fires. She was sitting in a chair beside the sheriff's desk.

"Kordelia, are you willing to testify that Billy Bob set the fires at the machine shop, the feed store and the bakery?" the sheriff asked the pinch-faced woman sitting at the table.

She hesitated for a moment and then gave an abrupt nod. "Billy Bob laid all the groundwork. He used some special ingredients to set it up. Then after he left town, I lit the fires a day or so later." Her face softened, and she almost smiled. "They were beautiful fires, weren't they?"

Dina shuddered at her own memories of the horrible flames. There was nothing beautiful about fires that were designed to kill and destroy. What had unsettled Kordelia's mind?

The sheriff looked up from the notes he was writing and asked, "Why did you plan these fires with Billy Bob? What did you hope to gain?"

"Isn't it obvious?" The bitterness and hate returned to Kordelia's face. "I wanted to get rid of Dina Paxton once and for all. When Billy Bob couldn't do it, I decided to burn down the restaurant. I knew she'd risk anything to save her lover."

Gabe's arm tightened around Dina.

JD leaned forward and cleared his throat. "Why did you want her to die?"

The older woman's gaze narrowed. "It was Dina this and Dina that. For years, I've been the one who has kept this town running while she took all the credit. I was the one who balanced the books and paid the bills. Did I ever get any credit? Did people even notice?"

"You hated Dina because you were jealous of her position in the town?" Gabe asked.

"You still don't get it, do you?" Kordelia looked outraged. "Nothing I ever did deserved notice. But precious little Dina lost her husband, and everybody coddled her. She made a nice fat profit from selling the construction company and then became the town's wonderful fire-fighter hero. She had everything. But that still wasn't enough for her. Oh, no, then she had to set her sights on my brother, Ralph." Kordelia's eyes filled with venom and fury as she looked at Dina. "I've seen you leading Ralph on. He never would have started to gamble if he wasn't sniffing around you. All those gifts. Where did you think the money was coming from?"

Dina was at a loss. "I'm sorry, Kordelia, I had no idea. I accepted the gifts for kindness' sake only."

"Kindness!" Kordelia almost came out of her chair. "Kindness would have been to leave the old fool alone. You might have been able to bamboozle Ralph, but I know a hussy when I see one. I told Ralph you only wanted his money, but he wouldn't listen to me. You'd give him a cute little smile, and then he'd run to the store to buy another outlandish gift. He spent *my* money on you and that stupid dog of his. You both should have died!"

Shaken, Dina didn't protest when Gabe pulled her back.

"Ralph was spending money you didn't have?" JD asked with a frown, obviously trying to make sense out of her venom.

The older woman gave him a dirty look before she answered. "Ralph went to Las Vegas on a junket with the mayor and some of his friends. I'd warned him about gambling time and time again, but Ralph never listened. He always thought his luck would change."

"Ralph was a gambling addict?" the sheriff prompted her.

"The old fool lost money neither of us had. When he came home with his tail dragging between his legs, I borrowed the money from the city to cover his debts."

The mayor peered at her with concern. "Why didn't you come to me, Kordelia? I would have lent you the money."

Kordelia lifted her chin. "Ralph and I don't need charity. We're respectable people."

"Finish your story, Kordelia," the sheriff encouraged.

Kordelia's lips tightened. "The annual audit was due to take place in a few weeks and I didn't have the money to repay the town. I was working on a dual set of books two months ago when Billy Bob stopped by city hall. He always came to talk to me when he was paying a visit. He's a charming young man. Handsome, too." For the first time, Kordelia nearly smiled. It was an unusual expression—one Dina realized she'd seldom seen on the older woman's face. Obviously Billy Bob had used his charm effectively. "Before I knew it, I spilled the whole miserable story to him.

That's when Billy Bob came up with the golden opportunity to pay Dina back. Fire was the perfect tool for her comeuppance.''

"What was Billy Bob getting out of this?" the sheriff asked. "Money?"

She shook her head. "Revenge. He usually earned big money for doing his little jobs, as he called them. But the Sherman fires were personal. After Dina refused to marry him, he decided to take his revenge by stopping her from opening the craft store. He burned down the machine shop before I knew about his true profession." Her expression turned to scorn as she sneered at Dina. "He didn't really want to marry you, you know. You weren't woman enough for his tastes he said, but he figured that he had to get married sometime and knew you had some good money selling the construction company."

"Who sent the notes to the newspaper?" JD asked. "Was that you or Billy Bob?"

She lifted her chin proudly and straightened in the chair. "I did. And nobody even suspected it was me. You all just thought I was stupid, ugly and unimaginative. Poor, dumb Kordelia Simpson. But I was smarter than anyone thought. I fooled everyone, didn't I? I even made it look as if city hall was the arsonist's next target." She gave an eerie cackle and stared at Dina. "You were so stupid. Gullible. Just like I'd always suspected. You believed the city hall would be next to burn. I would never destroy it. It's the only building worth saving in this miserable town."

She started to laugh as she watched their expressions of disbelief. "I also shoved the wall over at the fire site. The wall would have killed her but *he* got in the way." She pointed a shaky finger at Gabe. "It should have worked. Damn you all, it should have worked."

Dina and Gabe left when Kordelia started crying with frustration and anger over her failed attempt to get rid of Dina.

Gabe drove Dina back to the farm. After she turned on the lights in the living room, she collapsed on the couch and looked up at Gabe. "I feel sorry for Kordelia. Her bitterness has twisted her mind. I think she was even jealous of her own brother.''

''I wouldn't feel too sorry for her,'' Gabe growled, and dropped down next to her. He pulled her into the crook of his arm. ''She could have killed this entire community with her dangerous stunts.''

Dina was still trying to fit all the pieces of the puzzle together. She couldn't believe Kordelia had hated her for so long, even though everything made sense now. ''The bakery burned the same night that I went to the movies with Ralph. I just can't believe something so innocent could have created so much hate.'' And of course, every time Dina indicated to the mayor she was interested in purchasing a piece of property, Kordelia would have known because she was always in the city hall when Dina made the offer. ''If only I'd realized—''

Gabe just shook his head. ''Was there a history of mental illness in her family?''

Dina frowned. ''I don't remember much about her family, but her father died when I was a little girl. Everybody called him Crazy LeRoy because he was always talking to himself and liked to sleep in the bushes.'' She shook her head sadly. ''Why didn't we see how mixed up Kordelia was? Why did I accept those gifts from Ralph?''

''There was no way you could have known she considered you her rival for the town's attention. You can't take the blame, either, for Ralph's gambling problem. Those gaudy baubles he bought couldn't have cost more than a couple of bucks a piece. Most of the money he took from Kordelia he probably just gambled away but told Kordelia he'd bought you something.'' His assertion brooked no arguments. ''There was nothing you could have done to change what happened. Kordelia created her own problems and used you as a scapegoat.''

Dina squeezed her eyes shut, the memory of the past few hours sweeping through her. ''I'm not sure I can forgive her for thinking you and the restaurant were expendable.''

Gabe squeezed her hand, understanding her terror and relating it to his own. ''She was in more danger than I was.

She almost died when she became confused in the smoke and ended up in the closet.''

Dina would never forget the rush of horror when she realized Gabe was trapped inside the apartment. The smoke could have killed him long before she'd reached him. She shivered. ''You shouldn't have been in that building.''

He pulled her closer to his side, as if he never wanted her to move or be apart from him again. ''I shouldn't have left you here alone. It wasn't your fault.''

She refused to let him take the blame for her own spineless action. ''My fears drove you away from the farm.''

''You didn't push me. We both were responsible.'' He stroked her cheek and tipped her face toward him. His gentle caress brought a few tears to her eyes. He brushed them away with his thumb. ''I thought my life had stopped when you jumped onto the landing and almost fell to the ground. I don't want to experience another moment like that as long as I live. You're not getting rid of me again.''

She tried to smile but couldn't. ''My life wouldn't have been worth living if I hadn't gotten to you in time.''

''Both of us received a gift.'' He cupped her face gently between his hands. The warmth of his touch reached through the coldness that had been centered around her heart for so long. He stroked her cheek. ''I want you. I don't want you to be a caricature of my mother or sister. You're the woman I want, just the way you are.''

''I'll hold you to that,'' she whispered, clinging to every word and every look. How could she ever have considered letting this man go? ''What about my fire fighting? I know you don't like it.''

''I'm not going to deny it scares the hell out of me sometimes.'' He gave her his honesty. That was the foundation they both needed. ''But I trust you not to take unnecessary chances.''

The fullness of her love expanded within her. ''You can count on it.'' How had she earned this much happiness? For a moment, her pleasure dimmed as she thought about what might have been. ''I could have ended up as bitter and disillusioned as Kordelia if you hadn't come into my life.''

Gabe shook his head. "You were never in any danger o being Kordelia. She wallowed in her own misery and con tinued to add to it. Her insane jealousy was never your fault You were just being you. You have always been a very lov ing person, continually giving to others. That specialnes: has blessed many lives."

She blinked back the moisture gathering in her eyes. " received more from everyone than I ever gave."

His love was deep and sure on his face. "Will you marr me, Dina?"

"What about children?" she asked, with a slight catch ir her voice. She couldn't imagine any greater satisfaction ir life than to share a child with Gabe. But she had to be stron; enough not to smother a child because of her fear of losin; him or her to an act of fate. Would Gabe have patience witl her? Her troubled gaze met Gabe's. "Children are an im portant emotional commitment for both a man and : woman."

"Yes, they are." His finger traced the sensitive hollov beneath her ear. "We don't have to make this decision now When we do, it'll be what we both want. Together."

She felt his understanding and the overwhelming strengtl of his love in his embrace. Whatever happened, they'd fac it together. A future with Gabe was a risk worth taking, an she knew whatever hand fate dealt them, she'd never regre loving Gabe.

Epilogue

Dina puttered around the spare bedroom that had been Gabe's room for a brief time eighteen months ago. Now, yellow gingham curtains replaced the heavy old drapes. Fresh white paint brightened two walls, while the remaining walls wore cheery pastel paper. The completed room produced a contented glow within her, but not enough for her to ignore the slight ache in her lower back.

"You're going to have swollen ankles again tonight if you don't sit down and prop up those feet," Gabe said as he walked up behind her.

She leaned against him, savoring the warmth and strength he offered so naturally. "I just couldn't wait to put up those pictures Janey and Christina painted for the baby. They go perfectly with the room, don't they?"

He turned her around in his arms. "They're fantastic. Our baby's going to be the luckiest child in town. A beautiful room and a gorgeous mom."

She sighed. "I have a feeling a real baby is going to be a lot different from the plastic dolls we used at the hospital parenting classes. This baby is going to think he's a guinea pig." Every day she prayed for a healthy baby and thanked

God for the miracle growing inside of her. There were times when she became anxious, but Gabe was always at her side to reassure her and bolster her spirits.

He tugged on her curls, which now rested on her shoulders. "We'll make mistakes just like every other parent. But we're in this together, and that's been a powerful combination so far. He's going to be thankful to have parents who love him like we do. That's all any child really needs and wants."

When they'd decided nine months ago to start a family, neither one of them had anticipated the blessed union of egg and sperm would occur so quickly. Gabe considered it a combination of potency and combustion, whereas Dina figured it was probably due more to the frequency of their lovemaking. Together they were incredible. They never seemed to get enough of one another. Every day and every moment was more precious than the one before.

Gabe had rebuilt the portion of the restaurant that had burned and had added a small gift shop in the back where Dina and local craftsmen sold their wares. Dina had also taken on a partner in her pottery business so she'd have more time to spend with her family. She'd finally bowed out of the numerous committees that had claimed her attention for three years, and no longer felt the need to be so involved. In actual truth, she found herself resenting the time away from Gabe. He was the center of her life, and she celebrated every moment they shared.

"Come on, I have something for you." Gabe dragged her out of the baby's room and down the hall to their bedroom, where he made her sit down on the bed.

"What is it?" she asked.

He handed her an envelope. "Susan and Brenda sent us a list of parenting tips plus phone numbers where they can be reached any time of the day or night when we need advice or just a listening ear."

Dina swallowed and her eyes brimmed with tears. "All this love is overwhelming. I'm not sure I can handle much more."

"Are you going to miss not being a volunteer fire fighter for the next few months?" Gabe watched her with grave concern.

She knew he still worried about her, but his protectiveness gave her a feeling of security and contentment. Neither of them could forget the fragility of life nor the responsibility each one had toward the other's happiness. She patted her stomach. "There hasn't been a single fire in months. Besides, taking care of little Danny is going to keep me quite busy. I'll probably be learning some different rescue techniques."

Gabe wrapped her in his arms. He brought his lips down on hers, and she succumbed to the heat of his kiss just as she always did, ever since she'd been consumed by Gabe's fire.

* * * * *

Silhouette ROMANCE™

COMING NEXT MONTH

#1102 ALWAYS DADDY—Karen Rose Smith
Bundles of Joy—Make Believe Marriage
Jonathan Wescott thought money could buy anything. But lovely
Alicia Fallon, the adoptive mother of his newfound baby daughter,
couldn't be bought. And before he knew it, he was longing for the
right to love not only his little girl, but also her mother!

#1103 COLTRAIN'S PROPOSAL—Diana Palmer
Make Believe Marriage
Coltrain had made some mistakes in life, but loving Louise Blakely
wasn't one of them. So when Louise prepared to leave town, cajoling
her into a fake engagement to help his image *seemed* like a good idea.
But now Coltrain had to convince her that it wasn't his image he cared
for, but Louise herself!

#1104 GREEN CARD WIFE—Anne Peters
Make Believe Marriage—First Comes Marriage
Silka Katarina Olsen gladly agreed to a platonic marriage with
Ted Carstairs—it would allow her to work in the States and gain her
citizenship. But soon Silka found herself with unfamiliar feelings
for Ted that made their convenient arrangement very complicated!

#1105 ALMOST A HUSBAND—Carol Grace
Make Believe Marriage
Carrie Stephens was tired of big-city life with its big problems.
She wanted to escape it, and a hopeless passion for her partner,
Matt Graham. But when Matt posed as her fiancé for her new job,
Carrie doubted if distance would ever make her truly forget how
she loved him....

#1106 DREAM BRIDE—Terri Lindsey
Make Believe Marriage
Gloria Hamilton would only marry a man who cared for *her*, not just
her sophisticated ways. So when Luke Cahill trumpeted about his
qualifications for the perfect bride, Gloria decided to give Luke some
lessons of her own...in love!

#1107 THE GROOM MAKER—Lisa Kaye Laurel
Make Believe Marriage
Rae Browning had lots of dates—they just ended up marrying
someone else! So when sworn bachelor Trent Colton bet that she
couldn't turn him into a groom, Rae knew she had a sure deal. The
problem was, the only person she wanted Trent to marry was herself!

MILLION DOLLAR SWEEPSTAKES (III)

No purchase necessary. To enter, follow the directions published. Method of entry may vary. For eligibility, entries must be received no later than March 31, 1996. No liability is assumed for printing errors, lost, late or misdirected entries. Odds of winning are determined by the number of eligible entries distributed and received. Prizewinners will be determined no later than June 30, 1996.

Sweepstakes open to residents of the U.S. (except Puerto Rico), Canada, Europe and Taiwan who are 18 years of age or older. All applicable laws and regulations apply. Sweepstakes offer void wherever prohibited by law. Values of all prizes are in U.S. currency. This sweepstakes is presented by Torstar Corp., its subsidiaries and affiliates, in conjunction with book, merchandise and/or product offerings. For a copy of the Official Rules send a self-addressed, stamped envelope (WA residents need not affix return postage) to: MILLION DOLLAR SWEEPSTAKES (III) Rules, P.O. Box 4573, Blair, NE 68009, USA.

EXTRA BONUS PRIZE DRAWING

No purchase necessary. The Extra Bonus Prize will be awarded in a random drawing to be conducted no later than 5/30/96 from among all entries received. To qualify, entries must be received by 3/31/96 and comply with published directions. Drawing open to residents of the U.S. (except Puerto Rico), Canada, Europe and Taiwan who are 18 years of age or older. All applicable laws and regulations apply; offer void wherever prohibited by law. Odds of winning are dependent upon number of eligibile entries received. Prize is valued in U.S. currency. The offer is presented by Torstar Corp., its subsidiaries and affiliates in conjunction with book, merchandise and/or product offering. For a copy of the Official Rules governing this sweepstakes, send a self-addressed, stamped envelope (WA residents need not affix return postage) to: Extra Bonus Prize Drawing Rules, P.O. Box 4590, Blair, NE 68009, USA.

SWP-S895

SOMETIMES BIG SURPRISES COME IN SMALL PACKAGES!

Bundles
of Joy

BABY TALK
Julianna Morris

Cassie Cavannaugh wanted a baby, without the complications of an affair. But somehow she couldn't forget sexy Jake O'Connor, or the idea that he could father her child. Jake was handsome, headstrong, unpredictable...and nothing but trouble. But every time she got close to Jake, playing it smart seemed a losing battle....

Coming in August 1995 from

Silhouette ROMANCE™

BOJ3

As a *Privileged Woman,* you'll be entitled to all these *Free Benefits.* And *Free Gifts,* too.

To thank you for buying our books, we've designed an exclusive FREE program called *PAGES & PRIVILEGES™*. You can enroll with just one Proof of Purchase, and get the kind of luxuries that, until now, you could only read about.

*B*IG HOTEL DISCOUNTS

A privileged woman stays in the finest hotels. And so can you—at up to 60% off! Imagine standing in a hotel check-in line and watching as the guest in front of you pays $150 for the same room that's only costing you $60. Your *Pages & Privileges* discounts are good at Sheraton, Marriott, Best Western, Hyatt and thousands of other fine hotels all over the U.S., Canada and Europe.

*F*REE DISCOUNT TRAVEL SERVICE

A privileged woman is always jetting to romantic places. When <u>you</u> fly, just make one phone call for the lowest published airfare at time of booking—<u>or double the difference back!</u> PLUS—

you'll get a $25 voucher to use the first time you book a flight AND <u>5% cash back on every ticket you buy thereafter through the travel service!</u>

SR-PP4A

FREE GIFTS!

A privileged woman is always getting wonderful gifts.
Luxuriate in rich fragrances that will stir your senses (and his). This gift-boxed assortment of fine perfumes includes three popular scents, each in a beautiful designer bottle.   Truly Lace...This luxurious fragrance unveils your sensuous side. L'Effleur...discover the romance of the Victorian era with this soft floral. Muguet des bois...a single note floral of singular beauty.

YOURS FREE!

$50 VALUE

FREE INSIDER TIPS LETTER

A privileged woman is always informed. And you'll be, too, with our free letter full of fascinating information and sneak previews of upcoming books.

MORE GREAT GIFTS & BENEFITS TO COME

A privileged woman always has a lot to look forward to. And so will you. You get all these wonderful FREE gifts and benefits now with only one purchase...and there are no additional purchases required. However, each additional retail purchase of Harlequin and Silhouette books brings you a step closer to even more great FREE benefits like half-price movie tickets... and even more FREE gifts.

L'Effleur...This basketful of romance lets you discover L'Effleur from head to toe, heart to home.

Truly Lace...
A basket spun with the sensuous luxuries of Truly Lace, including Dusting Powder in a reusable satin and lace covered box.

Complete the Enrollment Form in the front of this book and mail it with this Proof of Purchase.